KU-711-920

Coming Through

Michael Ondaatje was born in Sri Lanka and lives in Toronto. His other books include *The Collected Works of Billy the Kid*, *The Cinnamon Peeler*, *Running in the Family*, the internationally celebrated *In the Skin of a Lion*, *The English Patient*, and, most recently, a collection of poetry, *Handwriting* (1998).

Also by Michael Ondaatje in Picador

The Collected Works of Billy the Kid

The Cinnamon Peeler

Running in the Family

In the Skin of a Lion

The English Patient

MICHAEL

ONDAATJE

COMING THROUGH SLAUGHTER

PICADOR

First published in Great Britain 1979 by Marion Boyars Publishing Ltd

This edition published 1984 by Picador
an imprint of Macmillan Publishers Ltd
25 Eccleston Place, London SW1W 9NF
Basingstoke and Oxford
Associated companies throughout the world
www.macmillan.co.uk

ISBN 0 330 28252 2

Copyright © Michael Ondaatje 1976, 1979

All rights reserved. No part of this publication may be reproduced, stored in or introduced into a retrieval system, or transmitted, in any form, or by any means (electronic, mechanical, photocopying, recording or otherwise) without the prior written permission of the publisher. Any person who does any unauthorized act in relation to this publication may be liable to criminal prosecution and civil claims for damages.

13 15 17 19 18 16 14 12

A CIP catalogue record for this book is available from the British Library.

Printed and bound in Great Britain by
Mackays of Chatham plc, Chatham, Kent

This book is sold subject to the condition that it shall not, by way of trade or otherwise, be lent, re-sold, hired out, or otherwise circulated without the publisher's prior consent in any form of binding or cover other than that in which it is published and without a similar condition including this condition being imposed on the subsequent purchaser.

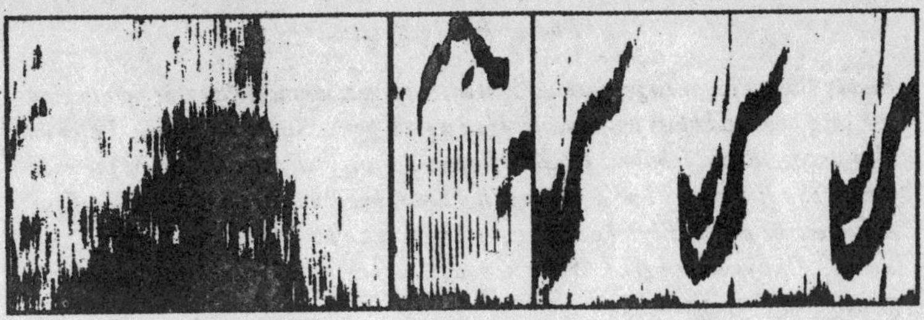

Three sonographs – pictures of dolphin sounds made by a machine that is more sensitive than the human ear. The top left sonograph shows a "squawk." Squawks are common emotional expressions that have many frequencies or pitches, which are vocalized simultaneously. The top right sonograph is a whistle. Note that the number of frequencies is small and this gives a "pure" sound – not a squawk. Whistles are like personal signatures for dolphins and identify each dolphin as well as its location. The middle sonograph shows a dolphin making two kinds of signals simultaneously. The vertical stripes are echolocation clicks (sharp, multi-frequency sounds) and the dark, mountain-like humps are the signature whistles. No one knows how a dolphin makes both whistles and echolocation clicks simultaneously.

Photo: Buddy Bolden

Buddy Bolden began to get famous right after 1900 come in. He was the first to play the hard jazz and blues for dancing. Had a good band. Strictly ear band. Later on Armstrong, Bunk Johnson, Freddie Keppard – they all knew he began the good jazz. John Robichaux had a real reading band, but Buddy used to kill Robichaux anywhere he went. When he'd take the people with him all the way down Canal Street. Always looked good. When he bought a cornet he'd shine it up and make it glisten like a woman's leg.

Louis Jones, 1909

1

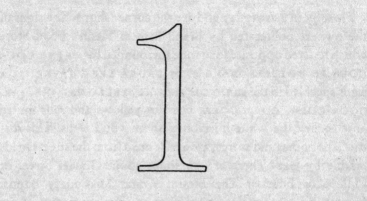

*

His geography.

Float by in a car today and see the corner shops. The signs of the owners obliterated by brand names. Tassin's Food Store which he lived opposite for a time surrounded by DRINK COCA COLA IN BOTTLES, BARG'S, or LAURA LEE'S TAVERN, the signs speckled in the sun, TOM MOORE, YELLOWSTONE, JAX, COCA COLA, COCA COLA, primary yellows and reds muted now against the white horizontal sheet wood walls. This district, the homes and stores, are a mile or so from the streets made marble by jazz. There are no songs about Gravier Street or Phillips or First or The Mount Ararat Missionary Baptist Church his mother lived next door to, just the names of the streets written vertically on the telephone poles or the letters sunk into pavement that you walk over. G R A V I E R. A bit too stylish for the wooden houses almost falling down, the signs the porches and the steps broken through where no one sits outside now. It is further away that you find Rampart Street, then higher up Basin Street, then one block higher Franklin.

But here there is little recorded history, though tales of 'The Swamp' and 'Smoky Row', both notorious communities where about 100 black prostitutes from pre-puberty to their seventies would line the banquette to hustle, come down to us in fragments. Here the famous whore Bricktop Jackson carried a 15 inch knife and her lover John Miller had no left arm and wore a chain with an iron ball on the end to replace it – killed by Bricktop herself on December 7, 1861, because of his 'bestial habits and ferocious manners'. And here 'One-legged Duffy' (born Mary Rich) was stabbed by her boyfriend and had her head beaten in with her own wooden leg. 'And gamblers carrying cocaine to a game'.

History was slow here. It was elsewhere in town, in the brothel district of Storyville, that one made and lost money – the black whores and musicians shipped in from the suburbs and the black customers refused. Where the price of a teenage virgin was $800 in 1860, where Dr Miles (who later went into the Alka Seltzer business) offered cures for gonorrhea. The women wore Gloria de Dijon and Marshall Neil roses and the whores sold 'Goofer Dust' and 'Bend-Over Oil'. Money poured in, slid around. By the end of the Nineteenth Century, 2000 prostitutes were working regularly. There were at least 70 professional gamblers. 30 piano players took in several thousand each in weekly tips. Prostitution and its offshoots received a quarter of a million dollars of the public's money a week.

Tom Anderson, 'The King of the District', lived between Rampart and Franklin. Each year he published a Blue Book which listed every whore in New Orleans. This was the guide to the sporting district, listing alphabetically the white and then the black girls, from Martha Alice at 1200 Customhouse to Louisa Walter at 210 North Basin, and then the octoroons. The Blue Book and similar guides listed everything, and at any of the mansions you could go in with money and come out broke. No matter how much you took with you, you would lose it all in paying for extras. Such as watching an Oyster Dance – where a naked woman on a small stage danced alone to piano music. The best was Olivia the Oyster Dancer who would place a raw oyster on her forehead and lean back and shimmy it down all over her body without ever dropping it. The oyster would criss-cross and move finally down to her instep. Then she would kick it high into the air and would catch it on her forehead and begin again. Or at 335 Customhouse (later named Iberville), the street he went crazy on, you could try your luck with French Emma's '60 Second Plan'. Whoever could restrain his orgasm with her for a whole minute after penetration was excused the $2 payment. Emma allowed the odd success to encourage others but boasted privately that there was no man she couldn't win. So no matter how much you took in you came out broke. Grace Hayes even had a pet raccoon she had trained to pick the pockets of her customers.

Anderson was the closest thing to a patron that Bolden had, giving him money for the family and sending him, via runner boys, two bottles of whisky a day. To the left of Canal Street was Dago Tony who, at the height of Bolden's popularity, sponsored him as well sending him Raleigh Rye and wine. And to the left of Canal are also the various homes of Bolden, still here today, away from the recorded history – the bleak washed out one-storey houses. Phillips, First, Gravier, Tassin's Food Store, taverns open all day but the doors closed tight to keep out heat and sunlight. Circle and wind back and forth in your car and at First and Liberty is a corner house with an overhang roof above the wooden pavement, barber stripes on the posts that hold up the overhang. This is N. Joseph's Shaving Parlor, the barber shop where Buddy Bolden worked.

*

He puts the towel of steam over a face. Leaving holes for the mouth and the nose. Bolden walks off and talks with someone. A minute of hot meditation for the customer. After school, the kids come and watch the men being shaved. Applaud and whistle when each cut is finished. Place bets on whose face might be under the soap.

*

N. Joseph's Shaving Parlor. One large room with brothel wallpaper left over from Lula White's Mahogany Hall. Two sinks with barber chairs in front of them, and along the wall several old donated armchairs where customers or more often just visitors sat talking and drinking. Pausing and tense when the alcohol ran out and drinking from the wooden coke racks until the next runner from Anderson or Dago Tony arrived, the new bottle travelling round the room including the half-shaved customer and the working Bolden, the bottle sucked empty after a couple of journeys, Bolden opening his throat muscles and taking it in so he was sometimes drunk by noon and would cut hair more flamboyantly. Close friends who needed cuts and shaves would come in early, well before noon.

In the afternoon a stray customer might be put in the chair and lathered by someone more sober and then Bolden would fight back into the room protesting loudly to his accusers that he had nerves of steel, and so cut hair once more, or whatever came in the way. Humming loud he would crouch over his sweating victim and cut and cut, offering visions of new styles to the tilted man. He persuaded men out of ten year mustaches and simultaneously offered raw steaming scandal that brought up erections in the midst of their fear. As the afternoon went on he elaborated long seductions usually culminating in the story of Miss Jessie Orloff's famous incident in a Canadian hotel during her last vacation. So friends came early to avoid the blood hunting razors of the afternoon. At 4 o clock in any case the shop closed down and he slept.

It was a financial tragedy that sleep sobered Bolden up completely, that his mind on waking was clear as an empty road and he began to casually drink again although never hard now for he played in the evenings. He slept from 4 till 8. His day had begun at 7 when he walked the kids a mile to school buying them breakfast along the way at the fruit stands. A half hour's walk and another 30 minutes for them to sit on the embankment and eat the huge meal of fruit. He taught them all he was thinking of or had heard, all he knew at the moment, treating them as adults, joking and teasing them with tall tales which they learned to sift down to the real. He gave himself completely to them during the walk, no barriers as they walked down the washed empty streets one on either side, their thin cool hands each holding onto a finger of his. Eventually they knew the politics of the street better than their teachers and he in turn learned the new street songs from them. By 8 they were at school and he took a bus back to Canal, then walked towards First, greeting everybody on his way to the shop.

What he did too little of was sleep and what he did too much of was drink and many interpreted his later crack-up as a morality tale of a talent that debauched itself. But his life at this time had a fine and precise balance to it, with a careful allotment of hours. A barber, publisher of *The Cricket*, a cornet player, good husband and father, and an infamous man about town. When he opened up the shop he was usually without customers for an hour or so and if there were any there they were usually 'spiders' with news for *The Cricket*. All the information he was given put unedited into the broadsheet. Then he cut hair till 4, then walked home and slept with Nora till 8, the two of them loving each other when they woke. And after dinner leaving for Masonic

Hall or the Globe or wherever he was playing. Onto the stage.

He was the best and the loudest and most loved jazzman of his time, but never professional in the brain. Unconcerned with the crack of the lip he threw out and held immense notes, could reach a force on the first note that attacked the ear. He was obsessed with the magic of air, those smells that turned neuter as they revolved in his lung then spat out in the chosen key. The way the side of his mouth would drag a net of air in and dress it in notes and make it last and last, yearning to leave it up there in the sky like air transformed into cloud. He could see the air, could tell where it was freshest in a room by the colour.

And so arrived amateur and accidental with the band on the stage of Masonic Hall, bursting into jazz, hurdle after hurdle. A race during which he would stop and talk to the crowd. Urging the band to play so loud the music would float down the street, saying 'Cornish, come on, put your hands through the window'. On into the night and into blue mornings, growing louder the notes burning through and off everyone and forgotten in the body because they were swallowed by the next one after and Bolden and Lewis and Cornish and Mumford sending them forward and forth and forth till, as he could see them, their bursts of air were animals fighting in the room.

*

With the utmost curiosity and faith he learned all he could about Nora Bass, questioning her long into the night about her past. Her body a system of emotions and triggers he got lost in. Every hair she lost in the bath, every dead cell she rubbed off on a towel. The way she went crazy sniffing steam from a cup of coffee. He was lost in the details, he could find no exact focus towards her. And so he drew her power over himself.

Bolden could not put things in their place. What thrilled him beyond any measure was that she, for instance, believed in the sandman when putting the children to bed whereas even the children didn't.

Quick under the covers, the sandman's coming down the street.

Where where show us.

He's just stopped to get a drink. And the children groaned inwardly but went to bed anyway. For three years a whore before she married Bolden she had managed to save delicate rules and ceremonies for herself.

But his own mind was helpless against every moment's headline. He did nothing but leap into the mass of changes and explore them and all the tiny facets so that eventually he was almost completely governed by fears of certainty. He distrusted it in anyone but Nora for there it went to the spine, and yet he attacked it again and again in her, cruelly, hating it, the sure lanes of the probable. Breaking chairs and windows glass doors in fury at her certain answers.

Once they were sitting at the kitchen table opposite each other. To his right and to her left was a window. Furious at something he drew his right hand across his body and lashed out. Half way there at full speed he realised it was a window he would be hitting and braked. For a fraction of a second his open palm touched the glass, beginning simultaneously to draw back. The window starred and crumpled slowly two floors down. His hand miraculously uncut. It had acted exactly like a whip violating the target and still free, retreating from the outline of a star. She was delighted by the performance. Surprised he examined his fingers.

Dragging his bone over town. Dragging his bone over town.
Dragging his bone over town. Dragging his
bone over town. Dragging his bone
over and over dragging his bone over town.
Then and then and then and then
dragging his bone over town

and then

dragging his bone home.

*

Dude Botley

Monday nights at Lincoln Park was something to see, especially when the madams and pimps brought their stables of women to hear Bolden play. Each madam had different colour girls. Ann Jackson featured mulatto, Maud Wilson featured high browns, so forth and so on. And them different stables was different colours. Just like a bouquet.

Bolden played nearly everything in B-Flat.

*

Nora Bass came home to find a man on her front step. Immaculate. Standing up as she approached, not touching her.

Hello Webb, come on in.

Thanks. Buddy must be out.

She half laughed. Buddy! And then looked quizzical at him. Then shook her head.

Yeah, you better come in Webb.

Alcohol burning down his throat as she tells him that Buddy went, disappeared, got lost, I don't know Webb but he's gone.

How long?

5 or 6 months.

Nora opening out the curtains so the light falls over him, the cup with the drink in front of his face, between them, shielding him from the story, gulping more down.

Jesus why didn't you tell me before, let me know.

I don't know you Webb, Buddy knows you, why didn't *he* tell you.

You should have told me.

You're a cop Webb.

He's not safe by himself, he's gone lost, with nothing – the *Cricket*, the band, the kids.

He didn't say anything.

He stands up and goes towards her.

Who was he with.

I don't know.

Tell me.

He has covered her against the window, leaning very close to her, like a lover.

You're shaking Webb.

He won't last by himself Nora, he'll fall apart. He's not safe by himself.

Why are you shaking?

He needs you Nora, who was he with last?

Crawley. Another cornet. He was playing with him in Shell Beach, north of here, never came back.

Just like that?

Just like that.

I could find him. Tell me about Crawley.

She moves his arm away holding the cloth of his sleeve and goes to the door, opens and leans against it. She is a mask, her hand against the handle, he almost doesn't realise what she is doing, then walks to the door, angry at her coldness.

Do you want me to?

Looking hard at him.

I'm not going to hire you Webb.

Jesus I don't want your fucking money!

I don't want your fucking compassion Webb. If you look for him then do it for yourself, not for me.

I'm very fond of him.

I know that Webb.

He's a great talent.

Silence from her, lifting her hand and moving it across the small dark living room and its old wallpaper and few chairs like a tired showman.

Most of the cash went down his throat or was given away.
You never did find your mother either did you?
What? ... No.

Sad laugh over her face as Webb moves past her. Webb steps backward off the doorstep with his hands in his pockets.

Are you with anybody now?
Long silence.
No.
He'll come back Nora. When he married you, before you two went to my cabin in Pontchartrain, he phoned and we talked for over an hour, he needs you Nora, don't worry he'll be back soon.

Nora closing the door more, narrow, just to the width of her face. Webb grins encouragement and walks slowly backwards down the four steps to the pavement. He has remembered the number of steps. He is wrong. Bolden will take two more years before he cruises home. Her door closes on him and he turns. Spring 1906.

*

He went down to Franklin and bought bananas. Hungry after seeing Nora. Webb got off the bus as soon as he saw the first grocery store and bought six bananas, then a pound of nectarines. Put them in the large pocket of his raincoat and walked on downtown following the direction of the bus towards Lincoln Park. It was still about 8 in the morning. He ate watching the travel of people going both ways. For those who saw him it looked as if he had nothing to do. As it was he was trying to place himself casually in a mental position that was so high and irrelevant he hoped to stumble on the clues that were left by Bolden's disappearance.

It looked as if Bolden had no notion he was *not* coming back when he left for Shell Beach. Webb took much more seriously than others of his profession sudden actions and off hand gestures. Always found them more dangerous, more determined. Also he had discovered that Bolden had never spoken of his past. To the people here he was a musician who arrived in the city at the age of twenty-two. Webb had known him since fifteen. He could just as easily be wiping out his past again in a casual gesture, contemptuous. Landscape suicide. So perhaps the only clue to Bolden's body was in Webb's brain. Sleeping in childhood stories and now thrown into the future like an arrow. To be finished when they grew up. What was Bolden's favourite story? Whose moment of terror did he want to witness, Webb thought as he began the third banana.

*

Don't go 'way nobody

Careless love

2.19 took my babe away

Idaho

Joyce 76

Funky Butt

Take your big leg off me

Snake Rag

Alligator Hop

Pepper Rag

If you don't like my potatoes why do you dig so deep?

All the whores like the way I ride

Make me a pallet on your floor

If you don't shake, don't get no cake.

*

The Cricket existed between 1899 and 1905. It took in and published all the information Bolden could find. It respected stray facts, manic theories, and well-told lies. This information came from customers in the chair and from spiders among the whores and police that Bolden and his friends knew. *The Cricket* studied broken marriages, gossip about jazzmen, and a servant's memoirs told everyone that a certain politician spent twenty minutes each morning deciding which shirt to wear. Bolden took all the thick facts and dropped them into his pail of sub-history.

Looked at objectively *The Cricket* contained excessive reference to death. The possibilities were terrifying to Bolden and he hunted out examples obsessively as if building a wall. A boy with a fear of heights climbing slowly up a tree. There were descriptions of referees slashed to death by fighting cocks, pigs taking off the hand of a farmer, the unfortunate heart attack of the ninety year old Miss Bandeen who opened her door one night to let in her cats and let in someone's pet iguana instead. There was the freak electrocution of Kenneth Stone who stood up in his bathtub to straighten a crooked lightbulb and was found the next morning by his brother Gordon, the first reaction of Gordon being to turn the switch off so that Kenneth fell stiff to the floor and broke his nose. Whenever a celebrated murder occurred Bolden was there at the scene drawing amateur maps. There were his dreams of his children dying. There were his dreams of his children dying. There were his dreams of his children dying. And then there was the first death, almost on top of him, saved by its fictional quality and nothing else.

Bolden's marriage to Nora Bass had been a surprise to most of his friends. Webb, in Pontchartrain, continuing his career as police detective, received a long phone call from Bolden with the news. Webb offered them his cabin which they could use during the next month, so Bolden and Nora went there. Eventually, after three weeks, Nora's mother drove up for a visit in her Envictor, her suitcase full of whisky. Since the death of Mr Bass she had two overwhelming passions – the drawings of Audubon, and an old python she had bought second-hand, retired from a zoo. And since the death of Mr Bass all her daughters had slipped successively into the red light district. Bolden in fact had slept with each of Nora's sisters in his time. Now he was formally married to one of them, the veil of suspicion had been removed from the mother's eyes, and the two of them would hold great drunk conversations together. A sparky lady. She would lecture him on the world of animals while he listened morosely studying her body for betrayals of her daughter's physical characteristics. The final stages of an evening's drunkenness would see her reaching into her suitcase to bring out the copies of Audubon drawings. Hardly able to talk around a slur now she'd interpret the damned birds, *damned*, as she saw them, for she was sure John James Audubon was attracted to psychologically neurotic creatures. She showed him the drawing of the Purple Gallinule which seemed to lean over the water, its eyes closed, with thoughts of self-destruction. You don't know that! Shut up, Buddy! She showed him the Prophet Ibis, obviously paranoid, that built its nest high up before floods came, and the Cerulean Wood Warbler drunk on Spanish Mulberry, and her favourite – the Anhinga, the Water Turkey, which she said would sit in the tree tops till disturbed and then plummet down into the river leaving hardly a ripple and swim off with just its eyes and beak cresting water – or if disturbed further would hide by submerging completely and walk along the river bottom, forgetting to breathe, and so drown. That's how they catch water turkeys, she said, scare them under water and then net their bodies when they float up a few minutes later, did you know that? Bolden shook his head. You tell a good story Mrs Bass but I don't believe you, you crazy woman, you're drunk you know that – you crazy woman. A week later Mrs Bass went for a drive and never came back. After lunch Buddy and Nora set out walking. They found the Envictor two miles down the road. Mrs Bass was sitting at the wheel and had been strangled.

There was much curiosity on Bolden's part. They had been away from news for nearly a month, god knew if there was a famous murderer in the area. His mind went into theories. Eventually he decided to take the car and drive to Pontchartrain and tell Webb about it. Nora refused to be left with a strangler around. They drove with the dead Mrs Bass in the front seat settling carefully into rigor mortis. At the turns however she would sometimes fall over onto Bolden's lap like a valuable statue, so Nora got in the front and Mrs Bass was put in the back seat. Covered with a tarp for diplomacy. Bolden parked outside the police station and asked for Webb. Nora went to a restaurant to get a meal.

Listen we've got a dead body outside.

What!

Yeah. Nora's mum. Strangled. We brought her in.

Other cops looked round. Webb took his feet off the desk and stood up.

Listen if you murdered her you should get rid of the body, you should've buried her, don't try to bluff it out.

Hell Webb, we didn't kill her, I liked the old lady, but it looks suspicious, she has a lot of cash we're gonna get, so how would it look if we buried her?

Right, and you can't claim the money without the body, so you'd *have* to bluff it.

We didn't do it you bastard.

Ok Ok I believe you, where's the body?

In the back seat. Under the tarp.

Ok go with Belddax here and bring it in.

Minutes later Belddax rushed in. Webb asked where Bolden was.

He's running down the road, sir.

What!

Someone stole the car.

This crisis deflated with investigation. Search parties went out looking for the car as well as a strangler in the Hill district. After two weeks nothing had been found. The Boldens who would have been reasonably wealthy had no chance of a will until the body was located. Advertisements were placed in *The Cricket* and the Pontchartrain papers for a lost Envictor and the goods therein. A year later Bolden got a letter from Webb.

Buddy –
I've solved the murder if not the disappearance. Not everyone agrees with me, and I wouldn't have thought of it if not for last week's newspaper. Enclosed.

> *St Tropez. France*
> The flamboyant and controversial 'dancer' Isadora Duncan died yesterday in another one of those dramatic situations that seemed to follow her all her life. Riding with a friend in his Bugatti, her silk scarf caught in the back wheel of the

> moving car and strangled her before the driver realised what was happening. The British Automobile Association has given out frequent warnings that this is a common danger to motorists. Miss Duncan was 49. For more of her life see 'SCARF' page 17.

You see what I'm getting at don't you. The old lady's pet snake is near her, taking in the breeze. Its tail somehow gets caught in a rear wheel. It quickly hangs onto the one thing close to it, her neck, this strangles her. After the car comes to a halt the snake who has been stretched badly but not killed uncoils and slides away. No trace of a weapon. If the snake was human it wouldn't get much more than manslaughter ... Sometimes Bolden I think I am a genius.

Webb

There were his dreams of his children dying.

*

The other kid came in with the news he's dead, sobbing, and he jumped and ran in one movement and caught the boy's shoulders WHO IS he heard himself weep out loud and being told floated into the kitchen picked up the wood handled knife with the serrated edge and pushed it again and again into his left wrist, then the open hand which was numb already, through the door and the police amazed at him his white shirt bloody looking at the cops who brought the news he'd always imagined each night – hit by a car, god. After the boy's words he hadn't heard a thing but his own screaming, went past the cop and leaned over the hot metal of the hood of the police truck, his face and his wet arm on it.

*

Crawley was losing weight and looking pale. He was fasting and the lines in his face were exaggerated. He sat in his chair drinking distilled water from a large bottle while Webb sat on the edge of the bed trying to get information. Now 10 a.m. He had got to him just before he started practising.

Give me half an hour. I'll be out by 10.30.
Who you?
I've just come from Nora. We're trying to find Buddy.

He tried offering Crawley a banana.

Banana, hell, I'm dieting. Just this special water.
Go on, take one, you look sick.
I can't. Jesus I'd like to. Do you know I haven't had a shit for a week?
How's your energy?
Slow ... this time I'm aiming for the tail of shit.
The tail of shit.
Yeah ... got to it once before. If you don't eat you see you finally stop shitting, naturally. And then about two weeks after that you have this fantastic shit, it comes out like a tornado. It's all the crap right at the bottom of your bowels, all the packed in stuff that never comes out, that always gets left behind.
Yeah? When did you last see Bolden?
Like someone removing a poker that's been up your arse all your life. It's fantastic. Then you can start eating again – is that a nectarine? I'll have a nectarine.
What was he doing when you last saw him?
He was on a boat.
Shit man, Bolden hated boats.
Listen, he was on a *boat*.

*

While Webb is talking to Crawley, this is what Bolden sees:

The woman is cutting carrots. Each carrot is split into 6 or 7 pieces. The knife slides through and hits the wood table that they will eat off later. He is watching the coincidence of her fingers and the carrots. It began with the colour of the fingers and then the slight veins on the carrot magnified themselves to his eyes. In this area of sight the fingers have separated themselves from her body and move in a unity of their own that stops at the sleeve and bangle. As with all skills he watches for it to fail. If she thinks what she is doing she will lose control. He knows that the only way to catch a fly for instance is to move the hand without the brain telling it to move fast, interfering. The silver knife curves calm and fast against carrots and fingers. Onto the cuts in the table's brown flesh.

*

'The only thing I can tell you Webb is about the last time I saw him. Last fall. He had never been on a boat before. Though god knows he's lived against the river all his life. But he was never on it. Anyway, the two of us and a couple of others went up to Shell Beach. We were supposed to play for three nights there. Usually we didn't play together but we liked each other's way and got on. There was very little money in the Shell Beach thing and each of the band was billeted with organisers. Bolden was to stay with a couple called the Brewitts – a pianist and his wife. You may have heard of him, Jaelin Brewitt, he used to be popular about five years ago...'

Spanish Fort, Shell Beach, Lake Pontchartrain,
Milneburg, Algiers, Gretna.
– All considered New Orleans suburbs.

[Milenburg Joys!]

Bolden lost himself then. Jaelin's wife, Robin, was very much part of the Shell Beach music world too, small enough in itself, but they got good musicians in and often. When he saw her he nearly fainted. After a party he went home with the Brewitts and pretended he was hungry so they wouldn't go to bed. Bolden was never much of an eater but he lied that he hadn't eaten for two days and so they sat there for three hours and he forced himself to eat and eat, taking twenty minutes with an egg squashed in a bowl and a drink in the hand. They sat till all tiredness was gone, the three of them, and about five in the morning they stood and groaned and went to bed. Then Bolden did a merciless thing. For the first time he used his cornet as jewelry. After the couple had closed their door, he slipped in a mouthpiece, and walked out the kitchen door which led to an open porch. Cold outside. He wore just his dark trousers and a collarless white shirt. With every sweet stylised gesture that he knew no one could see he aimed for the gentlest music he knew. So softly it was a siren twenty blocks away. He played till his body was frozen and all that was alive and warm were the few inches from where his stomach forced the air up through his chest and head into the instrument. Music for the three of them, the other two in bed, not saying a word.

Next morning Crawley was on the beach while Bolden got into the boat, a day cruiser, bobbing on the crowded Sunday water. He began to yell something at Crawley. Crawley called back. Bolden a hundred feet out with the Brewitts. They were shouting back and forth in musical terms. Crawley knew he was saying goodbye to his friend. He was saying goodbye to his friend.

'That was it ... I went back into town later that afternoon, he didn't show for the last two performances and didn't show at the train. I went over to the Brewitts the next day and Robin said he wasn't there. No one has seen or heard of him playing anywhere since. Shortly afterwards I heard the Brewitts had moved and haven't been seen either. It's been a case of everyone looking for Bolden and me saying I last saw him with the Brewitts and then people looking for the Brewitts. Nora didn't believe that. *Bolden*, she said, *on a boat*!'

*

He woke up and his mouth was parched. He didn't know what hour it was. The previous night of drink and talk with the Brewitts had made him lose the order of time. There was sunlight over part of the bed, his arm. He got some pants on and started down the hall towards the Brewitts' kitchen. Robin came round the corner at the other end. She was naked except for the sheet wrapped round her waist and trailing at her feet. Her long black hair on her shoulders and down her back. In each hand she was carrying a glass of orange juice, one for herself and one for Jaelin, walking back to their bedroom. She saw him and stopped, awkward, not knowing what to do. She looked at each of the glasses in her hands, then at him, and smiling shrugged. He stood still, where he was, as she walked past him, as she mouthed 'Morning' to him.

*

Webb twenty and Bolden seventeen when they worked in funfairs along the coast. Being financially independent for the first time they spend all their money on girls, and sometimes on women. They take rooms, stock beer, and gradually paste their characters onto each other. They spend a week alone building up the apartment in Pontchartrain. It is during this time that Webb and Bolden get to know each other. Afterwards, busy with women, their friendship is a public act of repartee, bouncing jokes off each other in female company. They live together for two years.

So Webb wanted to focus on that one week. And it was difficult for in that era, that time, it was Webb who was the public figure, Bolden the side-kick, the friend who stayed around. If others spoke of the two of them it was usually with surprise at what Webb could see in Bolden. The two of them after work busy with their own hobbies, Webb's curiosity making him move serene among his growing collection of magnets and Bolden practising for hours, strengthening his mouth and chest as he blew violently into a belled cornet. So the constant noise in Webb's ears was the muted howl in the other room. Till coming into Webb's room with beer and sweating Bolden would collapse in an armchair and say 'Tell me about magnets, Webb'. And Webb who had ten of them hanging on strings from the ceiling would explain the precision of the forces in the air and hold a giant magnet in his hands towards them so they would go frantic and twist magically with their own power and twitch and thrust up and swivel as if being thrashed jerking until sometimes the power that Webb held from across the room would break one of the strings and Webb would put his magnet at his foot and drag the smaller piece invisibly towards him or sometimes throw the magnet across the room halfway up the strings and the tied pieces of metal would leap up and jointly catch it in their smooth surfaces like a team of acrobats. Bolden would applaud and then they would drink.

After two years Bolden had gone to New Orleans and Webb stayed in Pontchartrain. Since then it was Bolden the musician that Webb heard stories of. It was Bolden who had jumped up, who had swallowed everything Webb was. Webb left with the roots of Bolden's character, the old addresses they passed through. A month after Bolden had moved Webb went to the city and, unseen, tracked Buddy for several days. Till the Saturday when he watched his nervous friend walk jauntily out of the crowd into the path of a parade and begin to play. So hard and beautifully that Webb didn't even have to wait for the reactions of the people, he simply turned and walked till he no longer heard the music or the roar he imagined crowding round to suck that joy. Its power.

*

Frank Lewis

It was a music that had so little wisdom you wanted to clean nearly every note he passed, passed it seemed along the way as if travelling in a car, passed before he even approached it and saw it properly. There was no control except the *mood* of his power ... and it is for this reason it is good you never heard him play on recordings. If you never heard him play some place where the weather for instance could change the next series of notes – then you *should* never have heard him at all. He was never recorded. He stayed away while others moved into wax history, electronic history, those who said later that Bolden broke the path. It was just as important to watch him stretch and wheel around on the last notes or to watch nerves jumping under the sweat of his head.

But there was a discipline, it was just that we didn't understand. We thought he was formless, but I think now he was tormented by order, what was outside it. He tore apart the plot – see his music was immediately on top of his own life. Echoing. As if, when he was playing he was lost and hunting for the right accidental notes. Listening to him was like talking to Coleman. You were both changing direction with every sentence, sometimes in the middle, using each other as a springboard through the dark. You were moving so fast it was unimportant to finish and clear everything. He would be describing something in 27 ways. There was pain and gentleness everything jammed into each number.

Where did he come from? He was found before we knew where he had come from. Born at the age of twenty-two. Walked into a parade one day with white shoes and red shirt.

Never spoke of the past. Simply about which way to go for the next 10 minutes.

God I was at that first parade, I was playing, it was a very famous entrance you know. He walks out of the crowd, struggles through onto the street and begins playing, too loud but real and strong you couldn't deny him, and then he went back into the crowd. Then fifteen minutes later, 300 yards down the street, he jumps through the crowd onto the street again, plays, and then goes off. After two or three times we were waiting for him and he came.

*

Shell Beach Station. From the end of the track he watched Crawley and the rest of the band get on the train. They were still half-looking around for him to join them from someplace, even now. He stood by a mail wagon and watched them. He watched himself getting onto the train with them, the fake anger relief on their part. He watched himself go back to the Brewitts and ask if he could stay with them. The silent ones. Post music. After ambition. As he watched Crawley lift his great weight up onto the train he could see himself live with the Brewitts for years and years. He did not have any baggage with him, just the mouthpiece in his pocket. He could step on the train or go back to the Brewitts. He was frozen. He woke to see the train disappearing away from his body like a vein. He continued to stand hiding behind the mail wagon. Help me. He was scared of everybody. He didn't want to meet anybody he knew again, ever in his life.

*

He left the station, went down to the small loin district of Shell Beach. Bought beer and listened to poor jazz in the halls. Listening hard so he was playing all the good notes in his brain his mouth flourishing whenever the players missed or avoided them. Had a dollar, less now. Enough for seven beers. Wearing his red shirt black trousers shoes. Stayed in the halls the whole day avoiding the bright afternoon sun which he could see past the open door of the bar, watching the band get replaced by others, ignoring the pick-ups who stroked his neck as they passed the tables. Dead crowd around him. He sat frozen. Then when his money was finished he went down to the shore and slept. Tried to sleep anyway, listening to the others there talk – where to hustle, the weather in Gretna. He took it in and locked it. In the morning he stole some fruit and walked the roads. Went into a crowded barber shop and sat there comfortable but didn't allow himself to be shaved walking out when it was his turn. Always listening, listening to the wet fluid speech with no order, unfinished stories, badly told jokes that he sober as a spider perfected in silence.

For two days picking up the dirt the grime from the local buses before he was thrown off, dirt off bannisters, the wet slime from toilets, grey rub of phones, the alley shit on his shoe when he crouched where others had crouched, tea leaves, beer stains off tables, piano sweat, trombone spit, someone's smell off a towel, the air of the train station sticking to him, the dream of the wheel over his hand, legs beginning to twitch from the tired walking when he lay down. He collected and was filled by every noise as if luscious poison entering the ear like a lady's tongue thickening it and blocking it until he couldn't be entered anymore. A fat full king. The hawk its locked claws full of salmon going under greedy with it for the final time. Nicotine from the small smokes he found burning into his nails, the socks thick with dry sweat, the nose blowing out the day's dirt into a newspaper. Asking for a glass of water and pouring in the free ketchup to make soup. Sank through the pavement into the music of the town of Shell Beach.

And then finding home in the warm gust of soup smells that came through pavement grids from the subterranean kitchens which kept him in their heat, so he travelled from one to another and slept over them at night drunk with the smell of vegetables, saved from the storms that came purple over the lake while he sat in the rain. Warm as a greenhouse over the grid, the heat waves warping, disintegrating his body. The shady head playing with the perfect band.

*

The ladies had come and visited them in their large brown painted apartment and their taste for women, diverse at first, became embarrassingly similar, both liking the tall brown ladies, bodies thin and long and winding, the jutting pelvis when naked. The relationships often moved over from Webb to Bolden or the other way.

Webb training in the police force, three years older, and Bolden a barber's apprentice emphasizing his ability to be an animated listener. Later on, after he moved, he continued listening at N. Joseph's Shaving Parlor. Here too he reacted excessively to the stories his clients in the chair told him, throwing himself into the situation, giving advice that was usually abstract and bad. The men who came into N. Joseph's were just as much in need of confession or a sense of proportion as a shave and Bolden freely gave bizarre advice just to see what would happen. He was therefore the perfect audience to these songs and pleas. Just take the money and put it on the roosters. Days later furious men would rush in demanding to speak to Bolden (who was then only twenty-four for goodness sake) and he would have to leave his customer and *that* man's flight of conversation, take the angered one into Joseph's small bathroom and instead of accepting guilt quickly suggest variations. Five minutes later Bolden would be back shaving a neck and listening to other problems. He loved it. His mind became the street.

Two years later Webb once more made a silent trip to New Orleans, partly to see how his friend was doing, partly to do with a Pontchartrain man being murdered there. Amazed from a distance at the blossoming of Bolden, careful again not to meet him. He finished the case in two days trying hard to keep out of Buddy's way for the man had died while listening to Bolden play. Two men had been standing at the bar separated by a third, a well dressed pianist. Buddy was on stage. Man A shot Man B with a gun, the pianist Ferdinand le Menthe between them leaning back just in time and disappearing before the first scream even began. Bolden seeing what happened changed to a fast tempo to keep the audience diverted which he had almost managed when the police arrived. Tiger Rag.

On his last night Webb went to hear Bolden play. Far back, by the door, he stood alone and listened for an hour. He watched him dive into the stories found in the barber shop, his whole plot of song covered with scandal and incident and change. The music was coarse and rough, immediate, dated in half an hour, was about bodies in the river, knives, lovepains, cockiness. Up there on stage he was showing all the possibilities in the middle of the story.

Among the cornet players that came after Bolden the one who was closest to him in volume and style was Freddie Keppard.

'When Keppard was on tour with the Creole Band, the patrons in the front rows of the theatre always got up after the first number and moved back.'

*

He found himself on the Brewitts' lawn. She opened the door. For a moment he looked right through her, almost forgot to recognize her. Started shaking, from his stomach up to his mouth, he could not hold his jaws together, he wanted to get the words to Robin or to Jaelin clearly. Whichever one answered the door. But it was her. Her hand wiping the hair off her face. He saw that, he saw her hand taking her hair and moving it. His hands were in his coat pockets. He wanted to burn the coat it stank so much. Can I burn this coat here? That was not what he wanted to say. Come in Buddy. That was not what he wanted to say. His whole body started to shake. He was looking at one of her eyes. But he couldn't hold it there because of the shake. She started to move towards him he had to say it before she reached him or touched him or smelled him had to say it. Help me. Come in Buddy. Help me. Come in Buddy. Help me. He was shaking.

2

*

Back then, Webb, there was the world of the Joseph Shaving Parlor. The brown freckles suspended in the old barber-shop mirror. This is what I saw in them. Myself and the room. Nora's plant that came as high as my shoulder. The front of the empty chair, the fake silver roller for the head to rest on. The wallpaper of Louisiana birds behind me.

The Joseph Shaving Parlor was the one cool place in the First and Liberty region. No one else within a mile could afford plants, wallpaper. The reason was good business. And the clue to good business, Joseph knew, was *ice*. Ice against the window so it fogged and suggested an exotic curtain against the heat of the street. The ice was placed on the wood shelf that sloped downwards towards the window at knee level. The ice changed shape all day before your eyes. Each morning I walked along Gravier to pick up the blocks of it and carried them into the parlor and slid them onto the slope. By 3.45 they had melted and drained through the boards into the waiting pails. At 4.00 I carried these out and threw the filmy water over the few plants to the side of the shop. The only shrubs on Liberty. The rest of the day I cut hair.

Cut hair. Above me revolving slowly is the tin-bladed fan, turning like a giant knife all day above my head. So you can never relax and stretch up. The cut hair falls to the floor and is swept by this thick almost liquid wind, which tosses it to the outskirts of the room.

I blow my nose every hour and get the hair-flecks out of it. I cough them up first thing in the morning. I spit out the black fragments onto the pavement as I walk home with Nora from work. I find pieces all over my clothes even in my underwear. I go through the evenings with the smell of shaving soap up to my elbows. It is there in my fingers as I play. The layers of soap all day long have made another skin over me. The cleanest in town. I can look at a face and tell how long ago it was shaved. I work with the vanity of others.

I see them watch their own faces for the twenty minutes they sit below me. Men hate to see themselves change. They laugh nervously. This is the power I live in. I manipulate their looks. They trust me with the cold razor at the vein under their ears. They trust me with liquid soap cupped in my palms as I pass by their eyes and massage it into their hair. Dreams of the neck. Gushing onto the floor and my white apron. The men stumbling with no more sight to the door and feeling even through their pain the waves of heat as they go through the door into the real climate of Liberty and First, leaving this ice, wallpaper and sweet smell and gracious conversation, mirrors, my slavery here.

*

So many murders of his own body. From the slammed fingernail to the sweat draining through his hair eventually bleeding brown into the neck of his shirt. That and Nora's habit of biting the collars of his shirt made him eventually buy them collarless. There was a strange lack of care regarding his fingers, even in spite of his ultimate nightmare of having hands cut off at the wrists. His nails chewed down and indistinguishable from the callouses of his fingers. He could hardly feel his lady properly anymore. Suicide of the hands. So many varieties of murder. After his child died in his dream it was his wrist he attacked.

*

I need a picture.
Thought you knew him.
I need it to show around.
Still – *shit* man who has pictures taken.
Bolden did, he mentioned one. Perhaps with the band.
You'll have to ask them. Ask Cornish.

But Cornish didn't have one though he said a picture had been taken, by a crip that Buddy knew who photographed whores. Bellock or something.

Bellocq.

He went down to the station and looked in the files for Bellocq's place. They knew Bellocq. He was often picked up as a suspect. Whenever a whore was chopped they brought him in and questioned him, when had he last seen her? But Bellocq never said anything and they always let him go.

Bellocq was out so he broke in and searched the place for the picture. Hundreds of pictures of whores in the cabinets. Naked and clothed, with pets or alone. Sad stuff. To Webb the only difference between these and morgue files was the others were dead. But there was nothing of Bolden. He sat down in the one comfortable armchair and eventually fell asleep. Buddy what the hell are you doing out there. You don't know what you're doing do ya. Hope Bellocq has the picture. I can't even remember what you look like too well. I'd recognize you but in my mind you're just an outline and music. Just your bright shirts that have no collars are there. Something sharp.

Something sharp was at his heart. Pressing. As he opened his eyes it pushed deeper and he jerked back into the chair. Bellocq was peering into his face out of the darkness. It must have been around two in the morning. Bellocq was still holding the camera case with his left hand and with the right hand the tripod, leaning his own chest against it so the three iron points were hard against Webb's body. Watch out man. Bellocq pressed harder.

What do you want. I've got no money.

I need a photograph.

None for sale.

Do you remember Bolden. He disappeared. I'm a friend. Trying to find him. Cornish told me you took a picture of the band.

Why don't you leave him, he's a good man.

I know I told you he was a friend. Can you take that hook off me and turn a light on in here. I'd like to talk to you.

Bellocq swung the tripod to his side in an arc. He didn't touch the lights or sit down but leaned against the tripod as if it were a crutch. You've got a nerve coming in here like this. Just like a cop.

Webb wanted Bellocq to talk. Bellocq began to walk around the room. He could hardly see the features on the small figure as it moved around him. There was something wrong with his legs and the tripod was now his cane. He had put the camera away carefully on a shelf. He walked round Webb several times expecting him to talk but the other was silent.

Cornish? He used to be in Bolden's band?

Yes.

Shitty picture.

Doesn't matter. I just need a picture with him in it.

I wouldn't want it getting around. Coughing over his tripod.

How'd you get to take it?

Long story. He knew some of the girls I used to do. He used to screw a lot and being famous they let him in. He used some of them to get stories for *The Cricket*. He paid them for that but not for the fucking. He was a kind man. He didn't treat you like a crip or anything. We'd talk a lot. It was him who got the girls to let me photograph them. They didn't like the idea at first. What was his real name?

Charlie.

Yeah. Charlie ... So I took the picture but I was using old film and it's no good.

Can I see it?

Don't have a print.

Make me one will you.

Ten minutes later he bent over the sink with Bellocq, watching the paper weave in the acid tray. As if the search for his friend was finally ending. In the thick red light the little man tapped the paper with his delicate fingers so it would be uniformly printed, and while waiting cleaned the soakboard in a fussy clinical way. The two of them watching the pink rectangle as it slowly began to grow black shapes, coming fast now. Then the sudden vertical lines which rose out of the pregnant white paper which were the outlines of the six men and their formally held instruments. The dark clothes coming first, leaving the space that was the shirt. Then the faces. Frank Lewis looking slightly to the left. All serious except for the smile on Bolden. Watching their friend float into the page smiling at them, the friend who in reality had reversed the process and gone back into white, who in this bad film seemed to have already half-receded with that smile which may not have been a smile at all, which may have been his mad dignity.

That's the best I can get. Keep the print.

Bellocq dried his hand of the acid by brushing it through his hair. Habit. From the window he watched the man who had just left waving the print to dry it as he walked. He hadn't asked him to stay longer. Lot of work tonight. He turned to the sink. He made one more print of the group and shelved it and then one of just Bolden this time, taking him out of the company. Then he dropped the negative into the acid tray and watched it bleach out to grey. Goodbye. Hope he don't find you.

He brought out the new film and proceeded to make about ten prints until they were all leaning against the counter, watching him. He hadn't told the man that much about Bolden. Hadn't told him he had pictures of Nora before she and Buddy were married. He looked in the files and found a picture of Nora Bass, five years younger. He hadn't seen her since the wedding – though it was no real wedding, just a party marriage. Buddy, who had given him free haircuts at Joseph's when there was no one there to disturb their talking. Sometimes late into the night, when he wasn't playing, Bolden would pull the blinds down and turn on the light of the shop so no one could look in and would warn him always about the acid in his hair. Except for cops this person tonight had been the first one here since Buddy. Not even Nora had come. He dropped her into the acid. No more questions. Watching the mist spill into her serious face.

*

The photographs of Bellocq. HYDROCEPHALIC. 89 glass plates survive. Look at the pictures. Imagine the mis-shapen man who moved round the room, his grace as he swivelled round his tripod, the casual shot of the dresser that holds the photograph of the whore's baby that she gave away, the plaster Christ on the wall. Compare Christ's hands holding the metal spikes to the badly sewn appendix scar of the thirty year old naked woman he photographed when she returned to the room – unaware that he had already photographed her baby and her dresser and her crucifix and her rug. She now offering grotesque poses for an extra dollar and Bellocq grim and quiet saying No, just stand there against the wall there that one, no keep the petticoat on this time. One snap to quickly catch her scorning him and then waiting, waiting for minutes so she would become self-conscious towards him and the camera and her status, embarrassed at just her naked arms and neck and remembers for the first time in a long while the roads she imagined she could take as a child. And he photographed that.

What you see in his pictures is her mind jumping that far back to when she would dare to imagine the future, parading with love or money on a beautiful anonymous cloth arm. Remembering all that as she is photographed by the cripple who is hardly taller than his camera stand. Then he paid her, packed, and she had lost her grace. The picture is just a figure against a wall.

*

Some of the pictures have knife slashes across the bodies. Along the ribs. Some of them neatly decapitate the head of the naked body with scratches. These exist alongside the genuine scars mentioned before, the appendix scar and others non-surgical. They reflect each other, the eye moves back and forth. The cuts add a three-dimensional quality to each work. Not just physically, though you can almost see the depth of the knife slashes, but also because you think of Bellocq wanting to enter the photographs, to leave his trace on the bodies. When this happened, being too much of a gentleman to make them pose holding or sucking his cock, the camera on a timer, when this happened he had to romance them later with a knife. You can see that the care he took defiling the beauty he had forced in them was as precise and clean as his good hands which at night had developed the negatives, floating the sheets in the correct acids and watching the faces and breasts and pubic triangles and sofas emerge. The making and destroying coming from the same source, same lust, same surgery his brain was capable of.

Snap. Lady with dog. Lady on sofa half naked. Snap. Naked lady. Lady next to dresser. Lady at window. Snap. Lady on balcony sunlight. Holding up her arm for the shade.

*

There were things Bellocq hadn't told him. He knew for he looked up from the street and saw the photographer in the window. He continued walking, the damp picture in his hand.

The connection between Bellocq and Buddy was strange. Buddy was a social dog, talked always to three or four people at once, a racer. He had no deceit but he roamed through conversations as if they were the countryside not listening carefully just picking up moments. And what was strong in Bellocq was the slow convolution of that brain. He was self-sufficient, complete as a perpetual motion machine. What could Buddy have to do with him?

The next day Webb knew more about Bellocq. The man worked with a team of photographers for the Foundation Company – a shipbuilding firm. Each of them worked alone and they photographed sections of boats, hulls that had been damaged and so on. Job work. Photographs to help ship designers. Bellocq, with the money he made, kept a room, ate, bought equipment, and paid whores to let him photograph them. What had Bolden seen in all this? He would have had to take time and care. Bellocq seemed paralysed by suspicions. He had let Buddy so *close*.

Webb walked around Bellocq for several days. Bellocq with his stoop, and his clothy hump, bent over the sprawled legs of his tripod. Not even bent over but an extension for he didn't have to bend at all, being 4 foot 11 inches. Bellocq with hair at the back of his head down to his shoulders, the hair at the front cut in a fringe so no wisps would spoil his vision. Bellocq sleeping on trains as he went from town to town to photograph ships, the plates wrapped carefully and riding in his large coat pockets. Something about the man who carries his profession with him always, like a wife, the way Bolden carried his mouthpiece even in exile. This is the way Bellocq moved. E.J. Bellocq in his worn, crumpled suits, but uncrumpled behind the knees.

In the no-smoker carriages his face through the glass, the superimposed picture, windows of passing houses across his mouth and eyes. Looking at the close face Webb understood the head shape, the blood vessels, the quiver to the side of the lip. Face machinery. HYDROCEPHALIC. His blood and water circulation which was of such a pattern that he knew he would be dead before forty and which made the bending of his knees difficult. To avoid the usual splay or arced walk which was the natural movement for people with this problem, he walked straight and forward. That is he went high on the toe, say of his right leg, which allowed the whole left leg enough space to move forward directly under his body like a pendulum, and so travel past the right leg. Then with the other foot. This also helped Bellocq with his height. However he did not walk that much. He never shot landscapes, mostly portraits. Webb discovered the minds of certain people through their bodies. Or through the perceptions that distinguished them. This was the stage that Bellocq's circulation and walk had reached.

*

In the heat heart of the Brewitts' bathtub his body exploded. The armour of dirt fell apart and the nerves and muscles loosened. He sank his head under the water for almost a minute bursting up showering water all over the room. Under the surface were the magnified sounds of his body against the enamel, drip, noise of the pipe. He came up and lay there not washing just letting the dirt and the sweat melt into the heat. Stood up and felt everything drain off him. Put a towel around himself and looked out into the hall. The Brewitts were out so he walked to his room lay down on the bed and slept.

When Robin came in he was on his back asleep, bedclothes and towel fallen off. She let her hair down onto his stomach. Her hair rustled against the black curls of his belly, then her mouth dropping its tongue here and here on his flesh, he slowly awake, her tongue the flesh explorer, her cool spit, his eyes watching her kneel over the bed. Then moving her face up to his mouth his shoulder.

Stay with us.

Does this change things?

Don't you think so? Don't you think Jaelin would think so?

I wouldn't feel different if I was him.

I can't do things that way Buddy.

She put her mouth at the hollow of his neck.

Your breath feels like a fly on me, about three or four of them on me.

Talk about the music, what you want to play.

You know Bellocq had a dog I'd watch for hours. It would do

nothing, all day it would seem to be sitting around doing nothing, but it would be *busy*. I'd watch it and I could see in its face that it was becoming aware of an itch on its ribs, then it would get up and sit in the best position to scratch, then it would thump away, hitting the floor more often than not.

Who was Bellocq.

He was a photographer. Pictures. That were like ... windows. He was the first person I met who had absolutely no interest in my music. That sounds vain don't it!

Yup. Sounds a bit vain.

Well it's true. You'd play and people would grab you and grab you till you began to – you couldn't help it – believe you were doing something important. And all you were doing was stealing chickens, nailing things to the wall. Everytime you stopped playing you became a lie. So I got so, with Bellocq, I didn't trust any of that ... any more. It was just playing games. We were furnished rooms and Bellocq was a window looking out.

Buddy –

She refused then to take off her clothes. She lay on top of him, kissing him, talking quietly to him. He could feel the material of her clothes all over his naked body, as if he were wearing them. His eyes closed. It could have been a sky not a ceiling above him.

Don't lean on that arm. Sorry. It got broken once.

She was conscious that while they spoke his fingers had been pressing the flesh on her back as though he were plunging them into a cornet. She was sure he was quite unaware, she was sure his mind would not even remember. It was part of a conversation held with himself in his sleep. Even now as she lay against his body in her red sweater and skirt. But she was wrong. He had been improving on *Cakewalking Babies*.

Passing wet chicory that lies in the field like the sky.

*

She. Again in the room, now in the long brown dress. Brown and yellow, no buttons no shoes and the click of the door as she leans against the handle, snapping shut so we are closed in with each other. The snap of the lock is the last word we speak. Between us the air of the room. Thick with past and the ghosts of friends who are in other rooms. She will not move away from the door. I am sitting on the edge of the bed looking towards the mirror. With her hands behind her. I must get up and move through the bodies in the air. To the first slow kiss in the cloth of her right shoulder into the skin of her neck, blowing my nervousness against the almost cold hair for she has been walking outside. My fingers into her hair like a comb till the hair is tight against the unused nerves between my fingers. The taste the pollen in her right ear, the soft circuit of her hearing wet with my spit that I send to her like a ship and suck back and swallow. This soft moveable limb on the side of her head.

I press myself into her belly. Her breath into my white shirt. Her cool breath against my sweating forehead so I can feel the bubbles evaporate. I lift her arms and leave them empty above us and bend and pull the brown dress up to her stomach and then up into her arms. Step back and watch her against the corner of my room her hands above her holding the brown dress she has lifted over her head in a ball. Turns her back to me and leans her face now against the dress she brings down to her face. Cool brown back. Till I attack her into the wall my cock cushioned my hands at the front of the thigh pulling her at me we are hardly breathing her crazy flesh twisted into corners me slipping out from the move and our hands meet as we put it in quick *christ* quickly back in again. In. Breathing towards the final liquid of the body, the liquid snap, till we slow and slow and freeze in this corner. As if this is the last entrance of air into the room that was a vacuum that is now empty of the other histories.

Lying here. Kept warm by her dress and my shirt over us. I am dry and stuck to her thigh. Joined by the foam we made. By the door, and the light and the air from the hall comes under the door. Sniff it. She hasn't taken one step further into my room. Dear Robin. I remember when I shook against you. The flavour of mouth. We are animals meeting an unknown breed. The reek, the size, where to find the right softness. Against this door. Coiled into each other under the brown and white cloth. Trying to come closer than that. A step past the territory.

*

Webb had spoken to Bellocq and discovered nothing. Had spoken to Nora, Crawley, to Cornish, had met the children – Bernadine, Charlie. Their stories were like spokes on a rimless wheel ending in air. Buddy had lived a different life with every one of them.

Webb circled, trying to understand not where Buddy was but what he was doing, quite capable of finding him but taking his time, taking almost two years, entering the character of Bolden through every voice he spoke to.

*

In fact Bellocq was more surprised than anyone when Buddy Bolden left. He had pushed his imagination into Buddy's brain, had passed it awkwardly across the table and entertained him, had seen him take it in return for the company, not knowing the conversations were becoming steel in his only friend. They had talked for hours moving gradually off the edge of the social world. As Bellocq lived at the edge in any case he was at ease there and as Buddy did not he moved on past him like a naïve explorer looking for footholds. Bellocq did not expect that. Or he could have easily explained the ironies. The mystic privacy one can be so proud of has no alphabet of noise or meaning to the people outside. Bellocq knew this but never bothered applying it to himself, he did not consider himself professional. Even his photographs were more on the level of fetish, a joyless and private game. Bellocq thought of this. Aware it was him who had tempted Buddy on. Buddy who had once been enviably public. And then this small almost unnecessary friendship with Bellocq. Bellocq had always thought his friend to be the patronising one, now he discovered it was himself.

*

Jaelin and Robin. Jaelin and Robin. Jaelin and Robin and Bolden. Robin and Bolden. There was this story between them. There was this deceit and then there was this honour between them. He wanted to tell that to Webb later.

The silence of Jaelin Brewitt understood them all. His minimal stepping out the door saying he would be back the next day. And he would be back not before the next day. All three of them talking for hours about things like the machinery of the piano, fishing, stars. This year, he told Bolden, there is a new star, the Wolf Ryat star. It should be the Wolf Star Bolden said it sounds better. It sounds better yes but that's not its real name. There were two people who found it. Someone called Wolf and someone called Ryat, Jaelin Brewitt said. There was that story between them. Later both of them realised they had been talking about Robin.

*

There is only one photograph that exists today of Bolden and the band. This is what you see.

Jimmy Johnson on bass	Bolden	Willy Cornish on valve trombone	Willy Warner on clarinet
	Brock Mumford on guitar	Frank Lewis on clarinet	

As a photograph it is not good or precise, partly because the print was found after the fire. The picture, waterlogged by climbing hoses, stayed in the possession of Willy Cornish for several years.

*

The fire begins with Bellocq positioning his chairs all the way round the room. 17 chairs. Some of which he has borrowed. The chairs being placed this way the room, 20′ by 20′, looks like it has a balcony running all the way around it. Then he takes the taper, lights it, stands on a chair, and sets fire to the wallpaper half way up to the ceiling, walks along the path of chairs to continue the flame until he has made a full circle of the room. With great difficulty he steps down and comes back to the centre of the room. The noise is great. Planks cracking beneath the wallpaper in this heat as he stands there silent, as still as possible, trying to formally breathe in the remaining oxygen. And then breathing in the smoke. He is covered, surrounded by whiteness, it looks as if a cloud has stuffed itself into the room.

Horror of noise. And then the break when he cannot breathe calm and he vomits out smoke and throws himself against the red furniture, against the chairs on fire and he crashes finally into the wall, only there is no wall any more only a fire curtain and he disappears into and through it as if diving through a wave and emerging red on the other side. In an incredible angle. He has expected the wall to be there and his body has prepared itself and his mind has prepared itself so his shape is constricted against an imaginary force looking as if he has come up against an invisible structure in the air.

Then he falls, dissolving out of his pose. Everything has gone wrong. The wall is not there to catch or hide him. Nothing is there to clasp him into a certainty.

*

Under the sunlight. I am the only object between water and sky. There can be either the narrow dark focus of the eye or the crazy chaos of white, that is the eyes wide, wishing to burn them out till they are stones.

In the late afternoon I walk back along the shore to the small house and it is against me dark and shaded. Robin and her friends. I am full of the white privacy. Collisions around me. Eyes clogged with people. Yesterday Robin in the midst of an argument flicked some cream on my face. Without thinking I jumped up grabbing the first thing, a jug full of milk, and threw it all over her. She stood by the kitchen door half laughing half crying at what I had done. She stood there frozen in a hunch she took on as she saw the milk coming at her. Milk all over her soft lost beautiful brown face. I stood watching her, the lip of the jug dribbling the rest onto the floor.

Jaelin and the others in the room silent. I very gently placed the jug on the table, such a careful gesture for I wanted her to see I was empty of all the tension. Then getting one of the big towels and placing it over her wet shirt. And then like a wise coward leaving the house till late evening when they had all gone to bed. When I got back she was still in the living room, almost asleep in the armchair.

Let's go for a swim. I want to get the milk out of my hair.
I'm sorry, try and forget it.
No I won't forget it, Buddy, but I know you're sorry.
Well it's just as well it happened.

Yeah, you'll be better for a few days. But which window are you going to break next, which chair.

Don't talk Robin.

You expect to come back and for me to say nothing? With Jaelin here?

Look you're either Jaelin's wife or my wife.

I'm Jaelin's wife and I'm in love with you, there's nothing simple.

Well it should be.

How do you think he feels. He said nothing, even when you went out. Do you really expect me to say nothing.

Yes. I'm sorry, you know that.

Ok ... let's swim Buddy.

She grins. And there is my grin which is my loudest scream ever.

In the water like soft glass. We slide in slowly leaving our clothes by the large stone. Heads skimming along the surface.

As long as I don't hurt you or Jaelin.

As long as I don't hurt you or Jaelin she mimics. Then beginning to imitate loons and swimming deeper, her head sliding away from me. Below our heads all the evil dark swimming creatures are waiting to brush us into nightmare into heart attack to suck us under into the darkness into the complications. Her loon laugh. The dull star of white water under each of us. Swimming towards the sound of madness.

*

See Tom Pickett.

Why?

Cos he, cos Buddy cut him up.

Why Pickett?

Go ask him.

Where'll I find him?

Don't know.

Tell me, Cornish.

Try Chinatown. Opium.

Was that why?

No.

Ok I'll find him.

Then as Webb is almost out of the door, Cornish saying

Listen what he'll tell you is true. I saw his face afterwards. You won't believe it but it's true.

Thanks Willy.

After a day he found Pickett in the room of flies. The air damp and thick. He had to practically sweep the flies off his face and hair.

Don't kill one you bastard or you'll be out, in fact get out'f here, willya.

What the fuck is all this. Not the dope but this mess. The flies.

I invite them in, ok? If you don't like it get out.

Cornish wouldn't know about this or Cornish would have told him. Cornish would never come here. Webb could hardly breathe without one going in his nose or into his mouth. Early evening and the windows closed, no breeze, just Tom Pickett and open food on plates around the room.

You're the first to come here since I started. Don't tell others.
I came to talk about Buddy.
I guessed. That's what everyone wants to talk about.

Pickett lying on the floor bed while Webb stood over him.

He did this. Pickett clapped his hands near his face so the flies left it for a moment and then settled back. Five or six scars cut into his cheeks. Pickett had been one of the great hustlers, one of the most beautiful men in the District.

Did they try to arrest him, is that why he went?
No.
Why did he go?
Don't know. I don't think it was this you see, he accepted what he did, he could do this and forgive himself. Shame wasn't serious to him.
How did it happen?
The flies moved over the roads on his face.

Nine o clock. Storm rain outside. *Cricket* work finished. Don't want to think. The kid has been around with the bottle and I haven't opened it yet. I watch the wall behind me in the mirror. Alone. Want to think.

Tom Pickett walks in. Black trousers and white shirt, the thunderstorm making it stick to his skin. Got time for a good haircut, Buddy? I think he said that, something like that. I was looking at the shirt speckled with long water drops, making it brown there. I get up and give him a small towel to dry his hair, unscrew the top and hand the bottle to him. Jesus it hasn't been touched, you sick? Shrug and point to the chair for him to sit in. Tells me, as always, exactly what he wants. Beautiful people are very conservative. And puts his feet up on the sink as usual. I lay the towel over his shirt and knot it at the back of his neck. He passes the bottle to me and I put it away.

'I started talking about his mood which was so quiet you know so fuckin strange for him and he still wouldn't say much. I guess if you want to find out what happened you should find out why he was like that. After a while I threw in a few cracks about the band playing too much and he didn't say much about that either. He was cutting the hair then, he was doing what I told him. But he was ... tense, you know. I started telling him this joke about, jesus I still remember what it was, aint that something? It was about the guy who is feeling good but everybody he meets tells him he looks terrible, well anyway he just said he'd heard it, so I shut up. I could see him in the mirror all the time. Then we started talking, I wasn't pushing him now. About my pimping. We always did that. That was our one real connection. Usually it was good talk cos even though he wasn't involved with the money he was a great hustler. I don't know if you knew that.'

'Yes.'

'Well he always had a sense of humour about it. He didn't come on like a preacher. So I was going on casual about trade, he'd done the left side of my head, and then he starts shouting at me, I mean real filth. So I thought it was a game right and I joked back. I thought he was joking. I started to heckle him about Nora and me, smiling at him in the mirror all the time and then he slips the towel round behind my neck and pulls back, pulls my neck back over the chair. He got his left arm under my chin – like this – then he opens the razor with his other hand, flicks it open in a movement like he was throwing it away and puts it in my shirt and slits it open in a couple of places. Once the shirt's open he starts shaving me up and down my front taking the hairs off. I wasn't moving or saying anything. Thought I'd keep still. Then he slices off my nipple. I don't think he meant to, was probably an accident. But that got me shouting. Then he lets go my neck and starts shaving my face very fast now small cuts now I was crying from the pain and the tears were going into the cuts, then I got my thumb into the wrist with the razor and got free, that's when I got really badly cut on the face, this one here. But I got loose and took a small chair against him.'

Right on my head. But I still have the razor and we stand looking at each other. The blood drooling off his chin onto the wet shredded shirt. He takes a quick look at himself in the mirror and the tears just rush out of his face. I am exhausted, sorry for him. Got no anger at him now. I'm finished I'm empty but I can't tell him. What the hell is wrong with me? And Pickett's face is hard waiting to come for me, looking around the room. With the chair he got me on the head with, he moves sideways to the sink. With the other hand he lifts the leather strop that has the metal hook on the end of it. He sways it out to the left and then sends it back slowly to the right and lands the hook in the centre of the mirror. $45. It falls onto the towel he has placed in the sink before. In large pieces which is what he wanted. I stand with the razor at the back of the room.

He picks up a large piece of mirror and skims it hard across the room at me. It hits the wall to the left of my shoulder but it came really fast and it scares me. I know he will slice me. He takes the next piece and jerks it at me twenty feet away and it comes straight for me. My neck. Is coming for me I'm dead I can't. Move. And then catches on a muscle of air and tilts up crashing above my head. Door opens near me. Nora. What! Stay back. And I run to him before he can get more and wave him from the sink with the razor. He holds me back with the chair in his left hand, with the right he swings the strop gets me hard on the left elbow. Broken. Just like that, no pain yet but I know it is broken. He swings the chair but it is too heavy for speed and I avoid it. Swings the strop and gets me on the knee. Numb but I can move it. Next time he swings the chair I drop the razor and wrestle it from him and push him backwards now able to keep the strop off but my left hand still dead. See Nora in another mirror. The parlor is totally empty except for the two of us and Nora shouting in a corner at the back screaming to us that we're crazy we're crazy.

Pickett's face swelled now, he cannot see too well over the puffs. Balance. His strop and my chair. I won't swing the chair. If I go off balance he will go for the head. My knee is stumbling, pain coming through. Can't feel my arm. Pickett swings and the strop tangles in the chair. I push hard hard he goes back the wood almost against his face that he doesn't want me to touch. Push again and he goes over the ice through the front window. A great creak as the thing folds over him like a spider web, he goes through, the hook of the strop pulls the chair and me frantic I won't let go and I come through too over the ice and glass and empty frame. And we are on the street.

Liberty. Grey with thick ropes of rain bouncing on the broken glass, Pickett on the pavement and now me too falling on the bad arm he kicks but there is no pain it could be metal. We scramble apart. Three feet between us, still joined by strop and chair, the rain thick and hard. His shirt which was red in the parlor now bloated and pink, the spreading cherry at his nipple. Exhausted. Silent. Battle of rain all around us. Nora screaming through the open window stop stop then climbs out herself and runs to the rack of empty coke bottles and starts throwing them between us. Smash Smash Smash. And some which don't break but roll away loud and we still don't move. Then she aims them at Pickett. Hits him on the foot and he steps back unconcerned still watching me then hits him on the side of the head and he gasps for she has hit a cut, the blood down his face. Shakes himself and drops the strop, moves backwards his hand over his eye, and then lopes down the street shouting out I tried to kill him.

So he leaves me Tom Pickett. Goes to tell my friends I have gone mad. Nora walking to me slowly to tell me I am mad. I put the chair down and I sit in it. Tired. The rain coming into my head. Nora into my head. Tom Pickett at the end of Liberty shouts at me shaking his arms, waving at me, my wife's ex-lover, ex-pimp, sit facing Tom Pickett who was beautiful. Nora strokes my arm, don't tell her I can't feel her fingers. Her anger or her pity. The rain like so many little windows going down around us.

*

Brock Mumford

'He was impossible during that time, before he went. I had a room on the fourth floor. Room 119A, where we were yesterday. I was avoiding people. A lot of fuss about Buddy at this time. Band was breaking up and I was being used as the go-between, made to decide who was being unfair *this* time *that* time. So I just stopped going out during the day cos I'd be sure to run into one of them. Buddy was always shouting. In any argument he'd try to overpower you with yelling.

The last time I saw him ... The door downstairs was locked. Bell rang, I didn't want to answer and I just lay on the mattress smoking. Then minutes later he is tapping on the window, he had walked along the roof. In fact it was quite easy to do though he seemed so proud of himself I didn't tell him that. You took anything away from him in those days and he'd either start shouting or would go into a silent temper. He was a child really – though most of the time, and this is important, he was right. A lot of people wanted to knock him down at that time. The Pickett incident had made him unpopular. Buddy didn't leave at the peak of his glory you know. No one does. Whatever they say no one does. If you are at the peak you don't have time to think about stopping you just build up and up and up. It's only a few months later when it wears off – usually before anyone else realises it has worn off – that you start to go, if you are the kind that goes. But he was still playing fine....

He came in through the window and sat down on the foot of the bed I was lying on, and started talking right away. Just like you.

He sat down and he talked, god he talked, just complaining. It was about Frank Lewis or something. Someone had passed him on the street and not spoken, probably hadn't seen him. He went on and on. Then I started in saying how I was fed up too, that I didn't want to be judge any more to all these fights. I had my own problems. This was the first time I'd said this you know and I thought he might be interested but within a minute he started to show how bored he was of it. You know, just irritated, looking around the room, sniffing, clucking, as if he'd heard too much of this sort of thing. So I shut up and he went on. Then left about an hour later. By this time even I wasn't listening. Went out of the window saying they were probably watching the door.'

*

IF Nora had been with Pickett. Had really been with Pickett as he said. Had jumped off Bolden's cock and sat down half an hour later on Tom Pickett's mouth on Canal Street. Then the certainties he loathed and needed were liquid at the root.

Nora and others had needed the beautiful Pickett that much. To see her throwing bottles at Pickett in the rain to brush him away gave her a life all her own which he, Bolden, had nothing to do with. He was aware the scene on the street included a fight which did not include him. Pickett earlier so confident he knew her thoroughly, her bones, god he knew even the number of bones she had in her body.

Bolden imagined it all, the wet deceit as she hunched over him and knelt down under him or drank him in complex kisses. The trouble was you could see all the way through Pickett's mind, and so the moment he had said he had been fucking Nora Bolden believed him. In the very minute he was screening his laughter at Pickett's fantasies he believed him. Tom Pickett didn't have the brain to have fantasies.

He called Cornish. Everybody's ear. Made him drink and listen to him. LISTEN! Drinking so much the rhetoric of fury at everyone disintegrated into repetition and lies and fantasies. He dreamt up morning encounters between Nora and the whole band. Towards 4 o clock in the morning both of them were frozen with drinks in their hands, unable to move. Bolden was lying across three chairs muttering up to the ceiling.

Well I got to go Charlie.

NO! Don't go just tell me what you think of the bitch.

Well you don't know that, she's a beautiful lady Charlie.

Well what the hell – he mimicked – I'm a beautiful. Bursting into peals of laughter and sliding arms first onto the floor in order to laugh more fully. And then as Cornish had finally reached the door, Bolden on the floor saying, You know ... in spite of everything that happens, we still think a helluva lot of ourselves! And more laughter till Cornish was gone and his chest and his throat were tired from it.

He lay there crucified and drunk. Brought his left wrist to his teeth and bit hard and harder for several seconds then lost his nerve. Flopped it back outstretched. Going to sleep while feeling his vein tingling at the near chance it had of almost going free. Ecstasy before death. It marched through him while he slept.

*

For a while after that Frankie Dusen the trombonist took over some of Bolden's players. They called themselves the Eagle Band. Bunk Johnson, seventeen years old, took his place. And Bolden arrived at Lincoln Park and saw him playing there, up front centre, and just turned around and walked back through the crowd who stepped aside to let him pass. Dude Botley followed him and tells this story which some believe and which others don't believe at all.

'He steps out of the park like a rooster ignoring everybody, everything and goes up Canal. I trail him back to the barber shop. There's wood planks all over the broken glass window and he just rips one out and climbs in, steps off the ice-shelf onto the floor and paces around his arms out to the side like he's doing a cakewalk. I watch from across the street and soon he's just sitting there in one of the chairs looking into a mirror. Pretty dark there, not much light. There's light in the back of the shop and it pours in all over the floor of the shaving parlor and Bolden is restless as a dog in the chair. He shouldn't be there because he don't work there any more. This is about eight at night and I'm on the other side of the road shuffling to keep warm because it's cold and I should be dancing. I can even hear Lincoln Park over the streets.

I see him walk to the back of the parlor where the light is and he come back with a bottle and the cornet. He try first to drink but he begin crying and he put the bottle in the sink. The tears came to my eyes too. I got to thinking of all the men that dance to him and the women that idolize him as he used to strut up and down the streets. Where are they now I say to myself. Then I hear

Bolden's cornet, very quiet, and I move across the street, closer. There he is, relaxed back in a chair blowing that silver softly, just above a whisper and I see he's got the hat over the bell of the horn ... Thought I knew his blues before, and the hymns at funerals, but what he is playing now is real strange and I listen careful for he's playing something that sounds like both. I cannot make out the tune and then I catch on. He's mixing them up. He's playing the blues and the hymn sadder than the blues and then the blues sadder than the hymn. That is the first time I ever heard hymns and blues cooked up together.

There's about three of us at the window now and a strange feeling comes over me. I'm sort of scared because I know the Lord don't like that mixing the Devil's music with His music. But I still listen because the music sounds so strange and I guess I'm hypnotised. When he blows blues I can see Lincoln Park with all the sinners and whores shaking and belly rubbing and the chicks getting way down and slapping themselves on the cheeks of their behind. Then when he blows the hymn I'm in my mother's church with everybody humming. The picture kept changing with the music. It sounded like a battle between the Good Lord and the Devil. Something tells me to listen and see who wins. If Bolden stops on the hymn, the Good Lord wins. If he stops on the blues, the Devil wins.'

*

4763 Callarpine Street. Where the Brewitts live.

Webb arrived in front of the house at 7.30 in the morning. He slept in the parked car till 9. Till he thought they would be awake. There would be Bolden and there would be Robin Brewitt. And maybe Jaelin Brewitt. Ugly trees on the lawn, he went by the side of the house and climbed the stairs to the first floor. Knocked at the door. No reply. He went into the apartment, could see no one. He knocked on a door in the hall and looked in. Robin Brewitt asleep in bed.

What?
Sorry. I'm looking for Buddy.
He's up somewhere. Maybe the bathroom.

He nodded and closed the door quietly. Went down the hall. Knocked on the bathroom door.

Yep!

And went in and found him.

He sat on the edge of the tub where his friend was having a bath. At first Bolden was laughing. He couldn't get over it. He wanted to know how. Webb gave him all the names. Nora. Cornish. Pickett. Bellocq. Bellocq! Yes Bellocq's dead now, killed himself in a fire. What do you mean killed himself in a fire? He started a fire round himself.

They could hear Robin through the wall in the kitchen. And that's Robin Brewitt? Bolden nodded into the water. And Jaelin Brewitt comes and goes. Bolden nodded. And your music. Haven't played a note for nearly two years. Thought about it? A little. You could train in the Pontchartrain cabin. I don't want to go back, Webb. You want to go back Buddy, you want to go back. Webb on the edge of the enamel talking on and on, why did you do all this Buddy, why don't you come back, what good are you here, you're doing nothing, you're wasting, you're –

Till Bolden went underwater away from the noise, opening his eyes to look up through the liquid blur at the vague figure of Webb gazing down at him gesturing, till he could hardly breathe, his heart furious wanting to leap out and Bolden still holding himself down not wishing to come up gripping the side of the tub with his elbows to stop him to stop him o god jesus leave me alone his eyes staring up aching, if Webb reaches down and tries to pull him up he will never come up he knows that, air! his heart empty overpowers his arms and he breaks up showering Webb, gulping everything he possibly can in.

Breathing hard, yes ok Webb ok ok ok. Hunched and breathing hard looking at the taps while Webb on his right tried to brush the wetness off his suit beginning to talk again and Buddy hardly listening to him, listening past him to Robin and the morning kitchen noises that he knew he would lose soon. Webb was releasing the rabbit he had to run after, because the cage was open now and there would always be the worthless taste of worthless rabbit when he finished.

Robin hit the door. Is he staying for breakfast, Buddy?

Silence. Like a huge, wild animal going round and round the bathroom. Just before he closed his eyes he saw her standing, years ago, holding two glasses of orange juice. Yes. He's staying for breakfast.

Passing wet chicory that lies in the fields like the sky.

Passing wet chicory that lies in the fields like the sky.

Passing wet chicory lies

like the sky,

like the sky like the sky like the sky

passing wet sky chicory

passing wet sky chicory lies

*

When he left we sat with the remains of breakfast. The two of us knew at precisely the same time. When Webb was here with all his stories about me and Nora, about Gravier and Phillip Street, the wall of wire barrier glass went up between me and Robin. And when he left we were still here, still, not moving or speaking, in order to ignore the barrier glass. God he talked and sucked me through his brain so I was puppet and she was a landscape so alien and so newly foreign that I was ridiculous here. He could reach me this far away, could tilt me upside down till he was directing me like wayward traffic back home.

Here. Where I am anonymous and alone in a white room with no history and no parading. So I can make something unknown in the shape of this room. Where I am King of Corners. And Robin who drained my body of its fame when I wanted to find that fear of certainties I had when I first began to play, back when I was unaware that reputation made the room narrower and narrower, till you were crawling on your own back, full of your own echoes, till you were drinking in only your own recycled air. And Robin and Jaelin brought me back to that open fright with the unimportant objects.

He came here and placed my past and future on this table like a road.

This last night we tear into each other, as if to wound, as if to find the key to everything before morning. The heat incredible, we go out and buy a bag of ice, crack it small in our mouths and spit it onto each other's bodies, her tongue slipping it under the skin of my cock me pushing it into her hot red fold. But we are already travelling on the morning bus tragic. Like the ice melting in the heat of us. Dripping wet on our chest and breasts we approach each other private and selfish and cold in the September heatwave. We give each other a performance, the wound of ice. We imagine audiences and the audiences are each other again and again in the future. 'We'll go crazy without each other you know.' The one lonely sentence, her voice against my hand as if to stop her saying it. We follow each other into the future, as if now, at the last moment we try to memorize the face a movement we will never want to forget. As if everything in the world is the history of ice.

Morning. Water has dried tight on my chest and stomach. I wake up crucified on my back in this bed. There is no need to turn. Blue cloud light in the room. There is no need to turn my head for Robin is gone. Already my body has unbuckled out into the space she left. Bending my left hand over my body and then crashing it down as hard as I can on her half of the bed. And it bounces against the sheet. And as I knew, she's gone.

*

He went to Webb's cottage on Lake Pontchartrain on a bus. His hands dead on his thighs and his body leaning against the window, the wet weather outside and this woman on his right in the dark dress who smiled as she took the seat, scribbling something on paper that she is hunched over. Her legs twitching now and then as if her brain is there.

He tried to take in the smell of her. The taste of her mouth in the next hotel room they passed along the road. He knew the shape of her body. As she would stand in front of him, the small breasts cold in the room, the heart of her. He went with her for months into the relationship, awkward first fights, the slow true intimacy, disintegration after they exchanged personalities and mannerisms, the growing tired of each other's speed. All this before they went one more mile – as she wrote on and he thought on into the heart and mind of her, not even glancing at her as she got off alone at Milneburg for she was an old friendship now and he could guess the expressions, her face for all the moments. Accidental lust on the bus carrying her new into his dead brain so even months later, years later, pieces of her body and character returned. What he wanted was cruel, pure relationship.

*

Got here this afternoon. Walk around remembering you from the objects I find. Books, pictures on the wall, nail holes in the ceiling where you've hung your magnets, seed packets on the shelf above the sink – the skin you shed when you finish your vacations. Re-smell your character.

Not enough blankets here, Webb, and it's cold. Found an old hunting jacket. I sleep against its cloth full of hunter sweat, aroma of cartridges. I went to bed as soon as I arrived and am awake now after midnight. Scratch of suicide at the side of my brain.

Our friendship had nothing accidental did it. Even at the start you set out to breed me into something better. Which you did. You removed my immaturity at just the right time and saved me a lot of energy and I sped away happy and alone in a new town away from you, and now you produce a leash, curl the leather round and round your fist, and walk straight into me. And you pull me home. Like those breeders of bull terriers in the Storyville pits who can prove anything of their creatures, can prove how determined their dogs are by setting them onto an animal and while the jaws clamp shut they can slice the dog's body in half knowing the jaws will still not let go.

All the time I hate what I am doing and want the other. In a room full of people I get frantic in their air and their shout and when I'm alone I sniff the smell of their bodies against my clothes. I'm scared Webb, don't think I will find one person who will be the right audience. All you've done is cut me in half, pointing me here. Where I don't want these answers.

*

I go outside and piss in your garden. When I get back onto the porch the dog is licking at the waterbowl trying to avoid the yellow leaves floating in it. With all the time in the world he moves his body into perfect manoeuvering position so he can get his tongue between the yellow and reach the invisible water. His tongue curls and captures it. He enters the house with me, the last mouthful pouring out of his jaws. Once inside he rushes around so the cold night air caught in his hair falls off his body.

The dog follows me wherever I go now. If I am slow walking he runs ahead and waits looking back. If I piss outside he comes to the area, investigates, and pisses in the same place, then scratches earth over it. Once he even came over to the wet spot and covered it up without doing anything himself. Today I watched him carefully and returned the compliment. After he had leaked against a tree I went over, pissed there too, and scuffed my shoe against the earth so he would know I had his system. He was delighted. He barked loud and ran round me excited for a few minutes. He must have felt there had been a major breakthrough in the spread of hound civilization and who knows he may be right. How about that Webb, a little sensa humour to show you.

*

Tired. Sulphur. When you're tired, the body thick, you smell sulphur. Bellocq did that. Always. Two in the morning three in the morning against the window of the street restaurant he'd rub a match on the counter and sniff it in. Ammonia ripping into his brain. Jarring out the tiredness. And then back to his conversations about everything except music, the friend who scorned all the giraffes of fame. I said, You don't think much of this music do you? Not yet, he said. Him watching me waste myself and wanting me to step back into my body as if into a black room and stumble against whatever was there. Unable then to be watched by others. More and more I said he was wrong and more and more I spent whole evenings with him.

The small tired man sitting on the restaurant bench or the barber chair never saying his scorn but just his boredom at what I was trying to do. And me in my vanity accusing him at first of being tone deaf! He was offering me black empty spaces. Revived himself with matches once an hour, wanted me to become blind to everything but the owned pain in myself. And so yes there is a need to come home Webb with that casual desert blackness.

Whatever I say about him you will interpret as the working of an enemy and what I loved Webb were the possibilities in his silence. He was just *there*, like a small noon shadow. Dear Bellocq, he was so short he was the only one who could stretch up in the barber shop and not get hit by the fan. He didn't rely on anything. He trusted nothing, not even me. I can't summarize him for you, he tempted me out of the world of audiences where I had tried to catch everything thrown at me. He offered mole comfort, mole deceit. Come with me Webb I want to show you something, no come with me I want to *show* you something. You come too. Put your hand through this window.

*

You didn't know me for instance when I was with the Brewitts, without Nora. Three of us played cards all evening and then Jaelin would stay downstairs and Robin and I would go to bed, me with his wife. He would be alone and silent downstairs. Then eventually he would sit down and press into the teeth of the piano. His practice reached us upstairs, each note a finger on our flesh. The unheard tap of his calloused fingers and the muscle reaching into the machine and plucking the note, the sound travelling up the stairs and through the door, touching her on the shoulder. The music was his dance in the auditorium of enemies. But I loved him downstairs as much as she loved the man downstairs. God, to sit down and play, to tip it over into music! To remove the anger and stuff it down the piano fresh every night. He would wait for half an hour as dogs wait for masters to go to sleep before they move into the garbage of the kitchen. The music was so uncertain it was heartbreaking and beautiful. Coming through the walls. The lost anger at her or me or himself. Bullets of music delivered onto the bed we were on.

Everybody's love in the air.

*

For two hours I've been listening to a radio I discovered in your cupboard of clothes. Under old pyjamas. You throw nothing away. Nightshirts, belts, some coins, and sitting in the midst of them all the radio. The wiring old. I had to push it into a socket, nervous, ready to jump back. But the metal slid in and connected and the buzz that gradually warmed up came from a long distance away into this room.

For two hours I've been listening. People talking about a crisis I missed that has been questionably solved. Couldn't understand it. They were not being clear, they were not giving me the history of it all, and I didn't know who was supposed to be the hero of the story. So I've been hunched up on the bed listening to voices, and then later on Robichaux's band came on.

John Robichaux! Playing his waltzes. And I hate to admit it but I enjoyed listening to the clear forms. Every note part of the large curve, so carefully patterned that for the first time I appreciated the possibilities of a mind moving ahead of the instruments in time and waiting with pleasure for them to catch up. I had never been aware of that mechanistic pleasure, that trust.

Did you ever meet Robichaux? I never did. I loathed everything he stood for. He dominated his audiences. He put his emotions into patterns which a listening crowd had to follow. My enjoyment tonight was because I wanted something that was just a utensil. Had a bath, washed my hair, and wanted the same sort of clarity and open-headedness. But I don't believe it for a second. You may perhaps but it is not real. When I played parades we would be going down Canal Street and at each intersection people would hear just the fragment I happened to be playing and it would fade as I went further down Canal. They would not be there to hear the end of phrases, Robichaux's arches. I wanted them to be able to come in where they pleased and leave when they pleased and somehow hear the germs of the start and all the possible endings at whatever point in the music that I had reached *then*. Like your radio without the beginnings or endings. The right ending is an open door you can't see too far out of. It can mean exactly the opposite of what you are thinking.

An abrupt station shut down. Voices said goodnight several times and the orchestra playing in the background collapsed into buzz again, a few yards away from me in your bedroom.

*

My fathers were those who put their bodies over barbed wire. For me. To slide over into the region of hell. Through their sacrifice they seduced me into the game. They showed me their autographed pictures and they told me about their women and they told me of the even bigger names all over the country. My fathers failing. Dead before they hit the wire.

There were three of them. Mutt Carey, Bud Scott, Happy Galloway. Don't know what they taught me for the real teachers never teach you craft. In a way the stringmen taught me more than Carey and his trumpet. Or Manuel Hall who lived with my mother in his last years and hid his trumpet in the cupboard and never touched it when anyone was around. It was good when you listened to Galloway bubble underneath the others and come through slipping and squealing into neighbourhoods that had nothing to do with the thumper tunes coming out of the rest. His guitar much closer to the voice than the other instruments. It swallowed moods and kept three or four going at the same time which was what I wanted. While the trumpet was usually the steel shoe you couldn't get out of because you led the music and there was an end you had to get to. But Galloway's guitar was everything else that needn't have been there but was put there by him, worshipful, brushing against strange weeds. So Galloway taught me not craft but to play a mood of sound I would recognize and remember. Every note new and raw and chance. Never repeated. His mouth also moving and trying to mime the sound but never able to for his brain had lost control of his fingers.

In mirror to him Carey's trumpet was a technician – which

went gliding down river and missed all the shit on the bottom. His single strong notes pelting out into the crowds, able to reach any note that he wished for but always reaching for the purest. He was orange juice he was exercise, you understand. He was a wheel on a king's coach. So that was technique.

Drawn to opposites, even in music we play. In terror we lean in the direction that is most unlike us. Running past your own character into pain. So they died eventually maybe suiciding for me or failing because of a lost lip who knows. Climbing over them still with me in the sense I have tried all my life to avoid becoming them. Galloway in his lovely suits playing his bubble music under shit bands – so precise off the platform so completely alone in his music he wished to persuade no one into his style, and forgotten by everyone who saw him. A dull person off stage. And he'd lie and make himself even duller to keep people away from him. Who remembers him? Even I forgot him for so long until now. Till you ask these questions. He slipped back into my memory as accidentally as a smell. All my ancestors died drunk or lost but Galloway continued to play till he died and when he failed to show up was replaced. Had a stroke during breakfast at sixty-five and was forgotten. So immaculate when he fell against his chair even the undertaker could not improve on him.

So I suppose I crawled over him.

And Scott who kept losing his career to neurotic women.

And Carey who lost his hard lip too young and slept himself to death with the money he made. Floating around the bars to hear good music, having a good time and then died. Attracted to opposites again, to the crazy music he chose to die listening to, bitching at new experiments, the chaos, but refusing to leave the table and go down the street and listen to captive jazz he himself had generated. A dog turned wild in pasture.

He was my father too in the way he visited me and Nora at the end. Not liking my music damning my music but moving in for a month or so before he died, trying to make passes at my pregnant wife by getting up early in the morning when she got up and I was still in bed or in a bath. Perhaps even hurt by me not bothering to be jealous because I took my time getting downstairs. We would fight about everything. Even the way I held the cornet or shouted out in the middle of numbers. And still he'd come every night and listen and be irritated and enjoy himself tremendously. And then one morning in the room he shared with my first kid he stayed in bed and shook and shook, unable to move anything except for those massive shoulders. Arms struck dead. Get the sweat out of my eyes get the sweat out of my eyes fuckit I'm going to die, and then dead in the middle of a shake. I leaned over his wet body and put an ear to his mouth wanting more than anything then to hear his air, the swirl of air in him but there was none. His open mouth was an old sea-shell. I turned my head slowly and kissed the soft old lips. I then went over the barbed wire attached to his heart.

*

The black dog I picked up a few miles south of your place has snuggled against me. No woman for over a month has been as close to my body as he is tonight. I got up to make a drink and returned to find him sitting on the sofa where my warmth had been. Dogs on your furniture, Webb. He is quite dirty and I'll bathe him tomorrow. Just dusty for the most part but there are pointed knots of mud under the belly – probably collected by going through wet evening grass. He is not used to living in houses I can tell, although he immediately climbs onto furniture. He is not used to softness and every few hours throughout the night he moves from chair to sofa and finally finds the floor to be the answer. I came back into the room and he looked up expecting me to reclaim my place. I've snuggled against his warmth. Have just bent over and notice his claws are torn.

The heat has fallen back into the lake and left air empty. You can smell trees across the bay. I notice tonight someone has moved in over there. One square of light came on at twilight and changed the gentle shape of the tree line, making the horizon invisible. Was annoyed till I admitted to myself I had been lonely and this comforted me. The rest of the world is in that cabin room behind the light. Everyone I know lives there and when the light is on it means they are there. Before, every animal noise made me suspect people were arriving. Rain would sound like tires on the gravel. I would run out my heart furious and thumping only to be surrounded by a sudden downpour. I would stand shaking, getting completely wet for over a minute. Then come in, strip all my clothes off and crouch in front of the fire.

Webb I'm tired of the bitching tonight. The loneliness. I really wanted to talk about my friends. Nora and Pickett and me. Robin and Jaelin and me. I saw an awful thing among us. And that was passion could twist around and choose someone else just like that. That in one minute I knew Nora loved me and then, whatever I did from a certain day on, her eyes were hunting Pickett's mouth and silence. There was nothing I could do. Pickett could just stand there and he had her heart balanced on his tongue. And then with Robin and me – Jaelin stood there far more intelligent and sensitive and loving and pained and it did nothing to her, she had swerved to me like a mad compass, aimed east east east, ignoring everything else. I knew I was hurting him and I screwed her and at times humiliated her in front of him, everything. We had no order among ourselves. I wouldn't let myself control the world of my music because I had no power over anything else that went on around me, in or around my body. My wife loved Pickett, I think. I loved Robin Brewitt, I think. We were all exhausted.

*

From the very first night I was lost from Robin.

The cold in my head and the cough woke me. Walking round your house making hot water grapefruit and Raleigh Rye drinks. That was the first night that was four weeks ago. And now too my starving avoiding food. Drunk and hungry in the middle of the night in this place crowded with your furniture and my muttering voice. Robin lost. Who slid out of my heart. Who has become anonymous as cloud. I wake up with erections in memory of Robin. Every morning. Till she has begun to blur into Nora and everybody else.

What do you want to know about me Webb? I'm alone. I desire every woman I remember. Everything is clear here and still I feel my brain has walked away and is watching me. I feel I hover over the objects in this house, over every person in my memory – like those painted saints in my mother's church who seem to always have six or seven inches between them and the ground. Posing as humans. I give myself immaculate twenty minute shaves in the morning. Tap some lotion on me and cook a fabulous breakfast. Only meal of the day. So I move from the morning's energy into the later hours of alcohol and hunger and thickness and tiredness. Trying to overcome this awful and stupid clarity.

After breakfast I train. Mouth and lips and breathing. Exercises. Scales. For hours till my jaws and stomach ache. But no music or tune that I long to play. Just the notes, can you understand that? It is like perfecting 100 yard starts and stopping after the third yard and back again to the beginning. In this way the notes jerk forward in a spurt.

Alone now three weeks, four weeks? Since you came to Shell Beach and found me. Come back you said. All that music. I don't want that way any more. There is this other path I beat the bushes away from with exercise so I can walk down it knowing it is just stone. I've got more theoretical with no one to talk to. All suicides all acts of privacy are romantic you say and you may be right, as I sit here at 4.45 in the middle of the night, sky beginning to emerge blue through darkness into the long big windows of this house. Here's an early morning ant crossing the table ...

Three days ago Crawley visited me. I made you promise not to say where I was but you sent him here anyway. He came in his car, interrupted my thinking and it has taken me a couple of days to get back. With a girl fan he came in his car and played some music he's working on, while she was silent and touching in the corner. I could have done without his music, I could have done with her body. Music quite good but I could have finished it for him, it was a memory. I wanted to start a fight. I was watching her while he was playing and I wanted the horn in her skirt. I wanted her to sit with her skirt on my cock like a bandage. My old friend's girl. What have you brought me back to Webb?

The day got better with the opening of bottles and all of us were vaguely drunk by the time they left and me rambling on as they were about to leave, leaning against the driver's window apologizing, explaining what I wanted to do. About the empty room when I get up and put metal onto my mouth and hit the squawk at just the right note to equal the tone of the room and that's all you do. Pushing all that into the car as if we had a minute to live as if we hadn't talked rubbish all day.

You learn to play like that and no band will play with you, he says.

I know. I want to get this conversation right and I'm drunk and I'm making it difficult.

Shouting into his car, standing on the pebble driveway, the sweat on me which is really alcohol gone through me and bubbled out. I said I didn't want to be a remnant, a ladder for others. So Crawley knowing, nodding. I ask him about Nora, tells me that she's living with Cornish. And I've always thought of her as sad Nora, and my children, all this soft private sentiment I forgot to explode, the kids who grow up without me quite capable, while I sit out this drunk sweat, thinking along a stone path. I am terrified now of their lost love. I walk around the car put my head in to kiss Crawley's girl whose name I cannot even remember, my tongue in her cool mouth, her cool circling answer that gives me an erection against the car door, and round the car again and look at Crawley and thank him for the bottles he brought. His brain with me for two days afterwards.

Alcohol sweat on these pages. I am tired Webb. I put my forehead down to rest on the booklet on the table. I don't want to get up. When I lift my head up the paper will be damp, the ink spread. The lake and sky will be light blue. Not even her cloud.

3

Interviewer: To get back to Buddy Bolden –
John Joseph: Uh-huh.
Interviewer: He lost his mind, I heard.
John Joseph: He lost his mind, yeah, he died in the bug house.
Interviewer: Yes, that's what I heard.
John Joseph: That's right, he died out there.

*

Travelling again. Home to nightmare.

The earth brown. Rubbing my brain against the cold window of the bus. I was sent travelling my career on fire and so cruise home again now.

Come. We must go deeper with no justice and no jokes.

All my life I seemed to be a parcel on a bus. I am the famous fucker. I am the famous barber. I am the famous cornet player. Read the labels. The labels are coming home.

*

Charlie Dablayes Brass Band

The Diamond Stone Brass Band

The Old Columbis Brass Band

Frank Welch Brass Band

The Old Excelsior Brass Band

The Algiers and Pacific Brass Band

Kid Allen's Father's Brass Band

George McCullon's Brass Band

And so many no name street bands
... according to Bunk Johnson.

*

So in the public parade he went mad into silence.

This was April 1907, after his return, after staying with his wife and Cornish, saying *sure* he would play again, had met and spoken to Henry Allen and would play with his band in the weekend parade. Henry Allen snr's Brass Band.

The music begins two blocks north of Marais Street at noon. All of Henry Allen's Band including Bolden turn onto Iberville and move south. After about half a mile his music separates from the band, and though the whole procession is still together Bolden is now stained untouchable, powerful, an 8 ball in their midst. Till he is spinning round and round, crazy, at the Liberty-Iberville connect.

By eleven that morning people who had heard Bolden was going to play had already arrived, stretching from Villiere down to Franklin. Brought lunches and tin flasks and children. Some bands broke engagements, some returned from towns over sixty miles away. All they knew was that Bolden had come back looking good. He was in town four days before the parade.

On Tuesday night he had come in by bus from Webb's place. A small bag held his cornet and a few clothes. He had no money so he walked the twenty-five blocks to 2527 First Street where he had last lived. He tapped on the door and Cornish opened it. Frozen. Only two months earlier Cornish had moved in with Bolden's wife. Almost fainting. Buddy put his arm around Cornish's waist and hugged him, then walked past him into the living room and fell back in a chair exhausted. He was very tired from the walk, the tension of possibly running into other people. The city too hot after living at the lake. Sitting he let the bag slide from his fingers.

Where's Nora?
She's gone out for food. She'll be back soon.
Good.
Jesus, Buddy. Nearly two years, we all thought –
No that's ok Willy, I don't care.

He was sitting there not looking at Cornish but up at the ceiling, his hands outstretched his elbows resting on the arms of the chair. A long silence. Cornish thought this is the longest time I've ever been with him without talking. You never saw Bolden thinking, lots of people said that. He thought by being in motion. Always talk, snatches of song, as if his brain had been a fishbowl.

Let me go look for her.
Ok Willy.

He sat on the steps waiting for Nora. As she came up to him he asked her to sit with him.

I haven't got time, Willy, let's go in.

Dragging her down next to him and putting an arm around her so he was as close to her as possible.

Listen, he's back. Buddy's back.

Her whole body relaxing.

Where is he now?
Inside. In his chair.
Come on let's go in.
Do you want to go alone?
No let's go in, both of us Willy.

She had never been a shadow. Before they had married, while she worked at Lula White's, she had been popular and public. She had played Bolden's games, knew his extra sex. When they were alone together it was still a crowded room. She had been fascinated with him. She brought short cuts to his arguments and at times cleared away the chaos he embraced. She walked inside now with Willy holding her hand. She saw him sitting down, head back, but eyes glancing at the door as it opened. Bolden not moving at all and she, with groceries under her arm, not moving either.

*

The three of them entered a calm long conversation. They talked in the style of a married couple joined by a third person who was catalyst and audience. And Buddy watched her large hip as she lay on the floor of the room, the hill of cloth, and he came into her dress like a burglar without words in the family style they had formed years ago, with some humour now but not too much humour. Sitting against her body and unbuttoning the layers of cloth to see the dark gold body and bending down to smell her skin and touching with his face through the flesh the buried bones in her chest. Writhed his face against her small breasts. Her skirt still on, her blouse not taken off but apart and his rough cheek scraping her skin, not going near her face which he had explored so much from across the room, earlier. When Cornish had still been there.

They lay there without words. Moving all over her chest and arms and armpits and stomach as if placing mines on her with his mouth and then leaned up and looked at her body glistening with his own spit. Together closing up her skirt, slipping the buttons back into their holes so she was dressed again. Not going further because it was friendship that had to be guarded, that they both wanted. The diamond had to love the earth it passed along the way, every speck and angle of the other's history, for the diamond had been earth too.

*

So Cornish lives with her. Willy, who wanted to be left alone but became the doctor for everyone's troubles. Sweet William. Nothing ambitious on the valve trombone but being the only one able to read music he brought us new music from the north that we perverted cheerfully into our own style. Willy, straight as a good fence all his life, none to match his virtue. Since I've been home I watch him and Nora in the room. The air around them is empty so I see them clear. They are for me no longer in a landscape, they are not in the street they walk over, the chairs disappear under them. They are complete and exact and final. No longer the every-second change I saw before but like statues of personality now. Through my one-dimensional eye. I left the other in the other home, Robin flying off with it into her cloud. So I see Willy and Nora as they are and always will be and I hunger to be as still as them, my brain tying me up in this chair. Locked inside the frame, boiled down in love and anger into dynamo that cannot move except on itself.

I had wanted to be the reservoir where engines and people drank, blood sperm music pouring out and getting hooked in someone's ear. The way flowers were still and fed bees. And we took from the others too this way, music that was nothing till Mumford and Lewis and Johnson and I joined Cornish and made him furious because we wouldn't let him even finish the song once before we changed it to our blood. Cornish who played the same note the same way every time who was our frame our diving board that we leapt off, the one we sacrificed so he could remain the overlooked metronome.

So because Willy was the first I saw when I got back I pretended to look through his eyes, the eyes Nora wanted me to have. So everyone said I'd changed. Floating in the ether. They want nothing to have changed. Unaware of the hook floating around. A couple of years ago I would have sat down and thought out precisely why it was Cornish who moved in with her why it was Cornish she accepted would have thought it out as I set the very type it was translated into. *The Cricket*. But I shat those theories out completely.

There had been such sense in it. This afternoon I spend going over four months worth of *The Cricket*. Nora had every issue in the bedroom cupboard and while she was out and the kids stayed around embarrassed to come too close and disturb me (probably Nora's advice – why doesn't she still hate me? Why do people forget hate so easily?) I read through 4 months worth of them from 1902. September October November December. Nothing about the change of weather anywhere but there were the details of the children and the ladies changing hands like coins or a cigarette travelling at mouth level around the room. All those contests for bodies with children in the background like furniture.

I read through it all. Into the past. Every intricacy I had laboured over. How much sex, how much money, how much pain, how much sweat, how much happiness. Stories of river-boat sex when whites pitched whores overboard to swim back to shore carrying their loads of sperm, dog love, meeting Nora, marriage, the competition to surprise each other with lovers. *Cricket* was my diary too, and everybody else's. Players picking up women after playing society groups, the easy power of the straight quadrilles. All those names during the four months moving now like waves through a window. So I suppose that was the crazyness I left. Cricket noises and Cricket music for that is what we are when watched by people bigger than us.

Then later Webb came and pulled me out of the other depth and there was nothing on me. I was glinting and sharp and cold from the lack of light. I had turned into metal at my mouth.

By breakfast the next day Cornish still hadn't returned so Buddy walked the kids to school, he was quiet but got them talking. Soon however numerous friends of his kids joined them on the walk. They were the ones who began conversations now and though the dialogue took him in there were codes and levels he was not allowed to be a part of as the group bounced loud and laughing towards the embankment. Hands in his pockets he strolled alongside them, his two kids dutifully sticking with him.

Hey Jace – this is my dad.
Oh yeah? Hi.

As they hit the embankment he impressed all by answering three complex dirty jokes in a row. Riddles he had heard years ago. Dug into his mind for further jokes he knew would be appreciated and which spread like rabies the minute they got into school.

Stanley, what's that note you're passing – bring it here.
It's a question Miss.
Bring it here.

Handed to her silently, creeping back to his desk.

What's this ... What's the diffrence, difference is spelled wrong Stanley, what's the difference between a nun praying and a young girl taking a bath? ... Well Stanley, stand up, what's the difference?

Rather not say Miss.

Come on come on, you know I like riddles.

You sure Miss.

Of course. As long as it's clever.

Oh it's clever Miss, Charles' dad told it.

Go on then.

Well. One has hope in her soul and one has soap in her –

STANNNNNLLLLLEEEEEEEEEEEEEEEEEEEEEEEY!

By the time they reached the school Bolden was a hero. He raked his memory for every pun and story. Finding out who the teachers were he revived old rumours about them. He suggested various tricks to drive a teacher out of the room, various ways to get a high temperature and avoid classes. As they approached the school the kids began to run from him fast into the yard to be the first there with the hoard of new jokes. He combed his fingers through his son's hair, kissed his daughter, and walked back. He avoided the areas he knew along Canal. Eventually he cut into Chinatown and asked about Pickett. No one knew of him, no one.

A guy with scars on his cheek, right cheek.

He was directed to the Fly King.

*

He was home then four days before the street parade. The first evening with Nora and Willy Cornish. The first night with Nora. The second morning with the children, late morning (perhaps) with Pickett. Pickett should not have been that difficult to find. He had at one time been a power. His room was on Wilson. Chinatown however was a terrible maze.

But Bellocq had been there photographing the opium dens, each scene packed with bunks that had been removed from sleeping compartments of abandoned trains, his pictures full of grey light which must have been the yellow shining off the lacquered woodwork. Cocoons of yellow silence and outside the streets which were intricate and convoluted as veins in a hand. Two squares between Basin and Rampart and between Tulane and Canal through which Bellocq had moved, never lost, and taken his photographs.

So Bolden had probably been there before, with him.

Parading around alone. I walk to Gravier north past Chinatown and then cut back to Canal, near Claiborne. Along the water. The mist has flopped over onto the embankment like a sailing ship. Others walking disappear into the white and the mattress whores have moved off their usual perch to avoid being hidden by the mist. They walk up and down, keep moving like sentries to show they haven't got broken ankles. The ones that have stand still and try to hide it. A quarter a fuck. The mist has helped them tonight. Normally now the pimps are out hunting the mattress whores with sticks. When they catch them they break their ankles. Women riddled with the pox, remnants of the good life good time ever loving Storyville who, when they are finished there, steal their mattress and with a sling hang it on their backs and learn to run fast when they see paraders with a stick. Otherwise they drop the mattress down and take men right there on the dark pavements, the fat, poor, the sadists who use them to piss in as often as not because the disease they carry has punched their cunts inside out, taking anything so long as the quarter is in their hands.

So their lives have become simplified by seeing all the rich and healthy as dangerous, and they automatically run when they see them. The ones who can run. The others drop their mattress and lie down and flick their skirts up, spread their legs with socks on, these ones who don't care who it is that's coming. If it's a pimp he's gonna check her for a swollen foot so she can't slip back to Storyville. These broken women so ruined they use the cock in them as a scratcher. The women who are called gypsy feet. And the ones not caught yet carrying their disease like coy girls into and among the rocks and the shallows of the river where the pimps in good shoes won't follow. But those who are lame thrusting their fat foot at you, immune from the swinging stick that has already got them swelled and fixed in a deformed walk, gypsy foot gypsy foot.

For them it is a good night. Standing like grey angels on the edge of the mist, stepping backward and invisible when they hear a fast rich walk. Like mine. God even mine, me with a brain no better than their sad bodies, so sad they cannot afford to feel sorrow towards themselves, only fear. And my brain atrophied and soaked in the music I avoid, like milk travelling over the border into cheese. All that masturbation of practice each morning and refusing to play and these gypsy feet wanting to play you but drummed back onto the edge of the water by your rich sticks and your rich laws. Bellocq showed me pictures he took of them long ago, he was crying, he burned the results. Thighs swollen and hair fallen out and eyelids stiff and dead and those who had clawed through to the bones on their hips. Rales. Dear small dead Bellocq. My brain tonight has a mattress strapped to its back.

Even with me they step into the white. They step away from me and watch me pass, hands in my coat pockets from the cold. Their bodies murdered and my brain suicided. Dormant brain bulb gone crazy. The fetus we have avoided in us, that career, flushed out like a coffin into the toilets and into the harbour. The sum of the city. To eventually crash into the boats going out to sea. Walk over the driblets of manure of the gypsy foot whores, they don't eat much, what they can beg or take from the half-formed weeds along the embankment. Salt in their pockets for energy. There is no horror in the way they run their lives.

Came home with just his face laughing at the jokes. Refused to enlarge stories as he used to. They noticed that, those who had known him before.

There were younger ones around now who had heard of him who wished to revive him but he easily turned conversations back onto them and their lives. Perhaps they were the eventual catalysts. Maybe. As it was they gradually heard of him being back and brought bottles of Raleigh Rye to leave on the doorstep, and Bolden just smiling and bringing the bottles in to Nora in the kitchen but not touching the cap, not drinking, not wishing to, now. Just talked gently and slowly with Nora, watching Nora get meals as he sat in the kitchen as if she was a sister he had never met since they were kids. And sleeping a lot.

On the third day old friends came in, shy, then too loud as they entertained him with the sort of stories he loved to hear, stories he could predict now. He sat back with just his face laughing at the jokes. It was like walking out of a desert into a park of schoolchildren. No one mentioned Pickett until he did and then there was silence and Bolden laughing out loud for the first time. And everyone in the room watching Buddy, waiting for any expression to move across his face, even a nerve.

No those visitors hadn't bothered him much. He liked to think of Pickett running down the road holding his scars like a dying dog. He still remembered the metal of the strop touch the mirror and both of them watching it fall, like a chopped sheet into the basin. No it was to Nora that the pain came, the people in the house watching him. Buddy's mind slipped through them. She saw him there and saw he wasn't even in the room, the only real muscle was his wink at her as some story was ending and she could see him getting his fucking grin ready. She wanted to collect everybody and kick them out of the room. Screw his serenity. Buddy knowing what he owed her and hadn't given her.

That night Willy Cornish went out again. Buddy was walking and came in at ten. It was after midnight when he wanted to go to sleep. One of the kids cried and without thinking he went into their room and lay on the edge of the bed his arm around the child. Act from the past. Charles jnr probably too old to want this. The cry was part of his sleep and he wasn't awake, just nuzzled into his father's body. Did Cornish do this?

He fell asleep, his fingers against his son's spine under the shirt. About an hour later he woke up and realised where he was. Took his jacket off and lay back in the old flannel shirt Nora had found for him to wear. Then heard Nora's 'Buddy' close to him and saw her sitting on Bernadine's bed, leaning forward. He got up and moved towards her.

You ok?
She shook her head slowly.
Is Willy out there?
No. He won't come back tonight Buddy.
Must be late.
1.30. I don't know.
He put his hand to the side of her face against her ear.
Please talk, Buddy.

He helps her off the bed and walks with her into the living room, his red arm loose over her shoulder.

She is on the sofa, he is in the chair. She lifts her knees up so her chin is resting on them. She is gazing at the floor between them.

Still love you Buddy ... I'm sorry. Not like it was before because I don't know you anymore but I care about you, love you as if you weren't my husband. I'm just sorry about this ... I feel sorrier for William. Jesus that red shirt on you, you look fabulous, you look really well aint that crazy that's all I can think of ... you look like a favourite shirt I lost.

They start giggling and soon are laughing across at each other.

Stop it Bolden, snorting back her laugh, we should be having a serious conversation.

His mouth on his wife's left ear. Feeling his wife's hands between their bodies unbuttoning the front of her dress. His own hands waiting and then into the cave of his wife's open dress, round to touch her back and sliding back to cover the breasts of his wife. His fingers recognizing the nipples, the appendix scar. He lies back with his head in her lap. Looking up at her. The home of his wife's mouth coming down on him.

*

With Bellocq on the street.

Walking with him to introduce him to whores. But I don't want you there when I do it. Ok Ok. Cos otherwise let's just go home. He was scared of Bolden's presence for the first time. He staggered at Buddy's side with the camera. You're sure? I just don't want you hanging round, just introduce me and say what I want. I know Bellocq I know. Yeah. Well you know what I mean.

He pulled Bellocq up the steps, the camera strapped across his back like a bow. He had seen it so often on his friend that whenever he thought of him his body took on an outline which included the camera and the tripod. It was part of his bone structure. A metal animal grown into his back. He pulled him up the steps, through the doors. You've got to get up these stairs man. Bellocq already exhausted began to climb them with Bolden. Man what a wallpaper, giggling as he climbed along the carpet runners that would take him to the paradise of bodies. He brushed his free hand against the blue embossed wallpaper. He saw a photograph of a girl sitting against it, alone on the stairs, no one around. Maybe a plate of food. The wallpaper would come out light grey. Up one flight, then another, his legs starting to ache. This ain't no joke is it man? No. One more and we're there.

Let me go in and talk to her first. Her? I thought I was going to meet them all. Yeah yeah but I just want to talk to Nora first ok.

He left Bellocq outside resting on the top steps carefully removing the camera off its sling. Listen I've got this friend who wants photographs of the girls. Same price as a fuck you know that Buddy. Ok, but I want to tell you about him first. Willya call the others in I don't want to say this more than once. He wasn't sure how to explain it. He wasn't even sure himself what Bellocq wanted to do. Listen this guy's a ship photographer – a burst of laughter – and just for himself, nothing commercial, he wants to get pictures of the girls. I don't know how he wants you to be for the picture, he just wants them. Nothing commercial ok. He's not weird or anything is he? No, he's a little bent in the body, something wrong with his legs. No one wanted to. Please, look I promised him, listen I even said no price this time, it's a favour, see he did a few things for me. You gonna be around Charlie? No I can't he doesn't want me to. Two of them left the room saying they were going back to sleep. Listen he's got a good job, he really does photograph ships and things, stuff for brochures. He's very good, he's not a cop, the idea coming into his mind that second as a possible fear of theirs. He's a kind man. Nobody wanted Bellocq and more went away. I'll give you a free knock anytime Charlie but not this. They went then and Nora shrugged sorry across the room. It's morning Charlie, they were all up late last night at Anderson's. All I could do was get them here. And they were watching the two of you arrive. He looked like something squashed or run over by a horse from up here.

Listen Nora you have to do this for me. Let him take some pictures of you. Just this once to show the others it's ok, I promise you it'll be ok. She had moved into the kitchenette and was looking for a match to light the gas. He came over, dug one out of his pocket and lit the row of hissing till they popped up blue, something invisible finding a form. He let her fill the kettle and put it on. Then he put himself against her back and leaned his face into her shoulder. His nose against the shoulder strap of her dress. Come out with me into the hall and meet him. Give him some of this tea. He's a harmless man. He put his head up a bit and watched the blue flame gripping the kettle. He was exhausted. He couldn't hustle for others, he didn't know the needs of others. He was fond of them and wanted them happy and was willing to make them happy and was willing to hear their problems but no more. He didn't know how people like Bellocq thought. He didn't know how to put the pieces of him together. He was too shy to ask Bellocq *why* he wanted these pictures or what kind they would be. Three floors up on North Basin Street he was nuzzling this lady. That's all he knew. His mind went blank against the flesh next to him.

What's he got on you? Nothing. He separated himself from her, picked up a knife and tapped against the small window of the kitchen, looking out. It was cold out, there was steam over the river. He had tried to get Bellocq to wear a coat when he had picked him up, but they had gone on, Bellocq cold and so trying to walk fast. He placed his palm against the glass and left the surface of his nerve pattern there. Rubbed it out. Turning he walked past her quickly through the door into the hall. As he was opening the door she said OK very fast. He turned and saw her leaning in the kitchen doorway with a cup in her hand. Then he opened the door to the stairs.

And then running down the stairs fast, almost crying, down two flights before he saw the figure in the main hall standing against the wallpaper looking up at him – the face pale and embarrassed. He must have heard them laughing in there, must have sat there for ten minutes and taken more than five minutes to walk down.

Yes or no, whatever it is, I'm not walking those stairs again.

I'll carry you up then. So decide. Shouting as he ran down.

Bugger you fuck you shit those voices carry you know.

I know. But it's ok. Nora will do it. He stood on the first stair looking at Bellocq, at Bellocq's sweating face. It's alright, she said she's gonna do it ok? She'll pose.

I heard them Buddy I *heard* them.

They didn't understand man, it's ok now come on. Come on.

Then he lifted the thin body of his friend and carried him up the three flights of stairs. Going slowly for he did not want to damage the camera or hurt the thin bones in the light body he was carrying. Still, he was tired and shaking and exhausted when he put him down on the top step.

She didn't speak to him about Bellocq. Not till this last night. He asked her about Bellocq and she told him what Webb had said, that Bellocq was dead. Died in a fire. This was about an hour after she found him sleeping in his red shirt with the children.

I only did that for you cos you know why?

No. Why?

Because you didn't know what to say, you didn't know how to argue me into it.

She threw in a taunt.

Tom Pickett could have hustled anyone to do what you asked in a minute.

No shit.

The last remark had flowed under him, he was thinking about Bellocq, crushed and scurrying to the front door that morning while the others had watched from the windows.

You didn't feel sorry for him?

I hated him Buddy.

But *why* ? He was so harmless. He was just a lonely man. You know he even talked to his photographs he was that lonely. Why do you hate him? You never even saw his pictures, they were beautiful. They were gentle. Why do you hate him?

She turned to face him.

Look at you. Look at what he did to you. Look at you. Look at you. Goddamit. Look at you.

*

The next morning his daughter saying, I had this awful dream. Mum made some food for us out of onions and hair and orange peels and we hated it and she said eat up it's good for you.

Coming down Iberville, warm past Marais Street, then she moves free of the crowd and travels at our speed between us and the crowd. My new red undershirt and my new white shiny shirt bright under the cornet. New shoes. Back in town.

Warning slide over to her and hug and squawk over her and shoulder her into the crowd. *Roar.* Between Marais and Liberty I just hit notes every 15 seconds or so Henry Allen worrying me eyeing me about keeping the number going and every now and then my note like a bird flying out of the shit and hanging loud and long. *Roar.* Crisscross Iberville like a spaniel strutting in front of the band and as I hit each boundary of crowd – *roar.* Parade of ego, cakewalk, strut, every fucking dance and walk I remember working up through the air to get it ready for the note sharp as a rat mouth under Allen's soft march tune.

But where the bitch came from I don't know. She moves out to us again, moving along with us, gravy bones. Thin body and long hair and joined by someone half bald and a beautiful dancer too so I turn from the bank of people and aim at them and pull them on a string to me, the roar at the back of my ears. Watch them through the sun balancing off the horn till they see what is happening and I speed Henry Allen's number till most of them drop off and just march behind, the notes more often now, every five seconds. Eyes going dark in the hot bleached street. Get there before it ends, but it's nearly over nearly over, approach Liberty. She and he keeping up like storm weeds crashing against each other. Squawk beats going descant high the hair spinning against his face and back to the whip of her head. She's

Robin, Nora, Crawley's girl's tongue.

March is slowing to a stop and as it floats down slow to a thump I take off and wail long notes jerking the squawk into the end of them to form a new beat, have to trust them all as I close my eyes, know the others are silent, throw the notes off the walls of people, the iron lines, so pure and sure bringing the howl down to the floor and letting in the light and the girl is alone now mirroring my throat in her lonely tired dance, the street silent but for us her tired breath I can hear for she's near me as I go round and round in the centre of the Liberty-Iberville connect. Then silent. For something's fallen in my body and I can't hear the music as I play it. The notes more often now. She hitting each note with her body before it is even out so I know what I do through her. God this is what I wanted to play for, if no one else I always guessed there would be this, this mirror somewhere, she closer to me now and her eyes over mine tough and young and come from god knows where. Never seen her before but testing me taunting me to make it past her, old hero, old ego tested against one as cold and pure as himself, this tall bitch breasts jumping loose under the light shirt she wears that's wet from energy and me fixing them with the aimed horn tracing up to the throat. Half dead, can't take more, hardly hit the squawks anymore but when I do my body flicks at them as if I'm the dancer till the music is out there. *Roar.* It comes back now, so I can hear only in waves now and then, god the heat in the air, she is sliding round and round her thin hands snake up through her hair and do their own dance and she is seven foot tall with them and I aim at them to bring them down to my body and the music gets caught in her hair, this is what I wanted, always, loss of privacy in the playing, leaving the stage, the rectangle of band on the street, this hearer who can throw me in the direction and the speed she wishes like an angry shadow. Fluff and groan in my throat, roll of a bad throat as we begin to slow. Tired. She still covers my eyes with hers and sees it slow and allows the slowness for me her breasts black under the wet light shirt, sound and pain in my heart sure as death. All my body moves to my throat and I speed again and she speeds tired again, a river of sweat to her waist her head and hair back bending back to me, all the desire in me is cramp and hard, cocaine on my cock, eternal, for my heart is at my throat hitting slow pure notes into the shimmy dance of victory, hair toss victory, a local strut, eyes meeting sweat down her chin arms out in final exercise pain, take on the last long squawk and letting it cough and climb to spear her all those watching like a javelin through the brain and down into the stomach, feel the blood that is real move up bringing fresh energy in its suitcase, it comes up flooding past my heart in a mad parade, it is coming through my teeth, it is into the cornet, god can't stop god can't stop it can't stop the air the red force coming up can't remove it from my mouth, no intake gasp, so deep blooming it up god I can't choke it the music still pouring in a roughness I've never hit, watch it *listen* it *listen* it, can't see I CAN'T SEE. Air floating through the blood to the girl red hitting the blind spot I can feel others turning, the silence of the crowd, can't see

Willy Cornish catching him as he fell outward, covering him, seeing the red on the white shirt thinking it is torn and the red undershirt is showing and then lifting the horn sees the blood spill out from it as he finally lifts the metal from the hard kiss of the mouth.

What I wanted.

Born 1876 ? A Baptist. Name is not French or Spanish.

He was never legally married.
Nora Bass had a daughter, Bernadine, by Bolden.
Hattie ———— had a son, Charles Bolden jnr, by him.

Hattie lived near Louis Jones' neighbourhood. (Jones born Sept 12, 1872, a close friend of Bolden).

Manuel Hall lived with Bolden's mum and taught him cornet. Hall played by note.

Other teachers were possibly Happy Galloway, Bud Scott, and Mutt Carey.

Mother lived on 2328 Phillip Street.

Bolden worked at Joseph's Shaving Parlor.

He played at Masonic Hall on Perdido and Rampart, at the Globe downtown on St Peter and Claude, and Jackson Hall.

April 1907 Bolden (thirty-one years old) goes mad while playing with Henry Allen's Brass Band.

He lived at 2527 First Street.

Taken to House of Detention, 'House of D', near Chinatown. Broken blood vessels in neck operated on.

June 1, 1907 Judge T.C.W. Ellis of the Civil District Court issued a writ of interdiction to Civil Sheriffs H.B. McMurray and T. Jones to bring Bolden to the insane asylum, just north of Baton Rouge. A 100 mile train ride on the edge of the Mississippi.

Taken to pre-Civil War asylum buildings by horse and wagon for the last fifteen miles.

Admitted to asylum June 5, 1907. 'Dementia Praecox. Paranoid Type.'

East Louisiana State Hospital, Jackson, Louisiana 70748.

Died 1931.

*

The sunlight comes down flat and white on Gravier, on Phillip Street, on Liberty. The paint on the wood walls has crumpled under the heat, you can brush it off with your hand. This is where he lived seventy years ago, where his mind on the pinnacle of something collapsed, was arrested, put in the House of D, shipped by train to Baton Rouge, then taken north by cart to a hospital for the insane. The career beginning in this street of the paintless wood to where he gave his brains away. The place of his music is totally silent. There is so little noise that I easily hear the click of my camera as I take fast bad photographs into the sun aiming at the barber shop he probably worked in.

The street is fifteen yards wide. I walk around watched by three men further up the street under a Coca Cola sign. They have not heard of him here. Though one has for a man came a year ago with a tape recorder and offered him money for information, saying Bolden was a 'famous musician'. The sun has bleached everything. The Coke signs almost pink. The paint that remains the colour of old grass. 2 pm daylight. There is the complete absence of him – even his skeleton has softened, disintegrated, and been lost in the water under the earth of Holtz Cemetery. When he went mad he was the same age as I am now.

The photograph moves and becomes a mirror. When I read he stood in front of mirrors and attacked himself, there was the shock of memory. For I had done that. Stood, and with a razorblade cut into cheeks and forehead, shaved hair. Defiling people we did not wish to be. He comes into the room, kneels in front of the mirror and sits on his heels. Begins to talk. Holds a blade between his first two fingers and cuts high onto the cheek. At first not having the nerve to cut deeper than scratches. When they eventually go deeper they look innocent because of the thinness of the blade. This way he brings his enemy to the surface of the skin. The slow trace of the razor almost painless because the brain's hate is so much. And then turning to his hair which he removes in lumps.

The thin sheaf of information. Why did my senses stop at you? There was the sentence, 'Buddy Bolden who became a legend when he went berserk in a parade ...' What was there in that, before I knew your nation your colour your age, that made me push my arm forward and spill it through the front of your mirror and clutch myself? Did not want to pose in your accent but think in your brain and body, and you like a weatherbird arcing round in the middle of your life to exact opposites and burning your brains out so that from June 5, 1907 till 1931 you were dropped into amber in the East Louisiana State Hospital. Some saying you went mad trying to play the devil's music and hymns at the same time, and Armstrong telling historians that you went mad by playing too hard and too often drunk too wild too crazy. The excesses cloud up the page. There was the climax of the parade and then you removed yourself from the 20th century game of fame, the rest of your life a desert of facts. Cut them open and spread them out like garbage.

They used to bury dogs on First Street. Holes in the road made that easy. While in Holtz Cemetery the high water table conveniently takes the flesh away in six months and others may be buried in the same place within a year. So for us you are here, not in Holtz with the plastic flowers in Maxwell House coffee tins or four inch plastic Christs stuck in cement or crosses so full of names they seem like ledgers of a whole generation.

The sun has swallowed the colour of the street. It is a black and white photograph, part of a history book.

*

House of Detention. Three needles lost in me. Move me over and in the fat of my hip they slip in the killer of the pain. And open my eyes and the nurse is there, her smiling rope face and rope neck. Awake Bolden? Nod. Look at each other and then she is off. No conversation. I can't sing through my neck. Every three hours I walk to the door for then she will come in carrying the needle in her sweet palm like an egg. Roll and dip and lose it in the bum. Go to sleep now. Nod. 7 am. I am given a bath. I sit up and she comes over unbuttons me at the back, pulls it over my shoulders. You see I can't use my arms. She pours the cold soap onto my chest and rubs hard across the nipple and hair. Smiling. Good? Nod. And then pulling my white dress further down and more cold soap in the circle of my crotch. As she leans against me there is the red morning on her face. Everyone who touches me must be beautiful.

Bolden's hand going up into the air
in agony.
His brain driving it up into the
path of the circling fan.

This last movement happens forever and ever in his memory

Interview with Lionel Gremillion at East Louisiana State Hospital.

Bolden's mother, Alice Bolden, wrote twice a month. Called him 'Charles'.

He died November 4, 1931 at the hospital.

His sister Cora Bolden Reed was notified when he died.

Geddes and Moss, Undertaking and Embalming Co. of New Orleans, took care of the body. Nov. 4, his sister sent telegram – 'PLEASE DELIVER REMAINS OF CHARLES BOLDEN TO J.D. GILBERT UNDERTAKING CO. BATON ROUGE TO BE PREPARED FOR BURIAL'.

Buried in unmarked grave at Holtz Cemetery after being brought from the Asylum through Slaughter, Vachery, Sunshine, back to New Orleans.

Reverend Sede Bradham, Protestant Chaplain at the Hospital, worked at the hospital in his youth. He had seen Bolden play in N.O. 'Hyperactive individual. When he blew his horn he kept walking around on the bandstand ... had tendency to go to a window to play to outside world.'

Dr Robard: 'He acted as a patient barber. Didn't publically proclaim himself as a jazz originator.'

Wasn't much communication between whites and blacks and so much information is difficult to find out. No black employees here.

Gremillion theorizing: 'He was a big frog, he had a following. Had a strong ego, his behaviour was eventually too erratic. Extroverted and then a pendulum swing to withdrawal. Suspiciousness. Paranoia. Possibly "an endocrine problem".'

Patients sometimes brought up by boat along Mississippi to St Francisville.

Typical Day:

Rose early. Summer 4.30 am. Winter 5 am.
If a person was in a closed ward he was returned there after breakfast. Bolden was probably in open and closed wards. If open ward he was given duties. His assigned duty was to cut hair. Lunch 11.30.

Recreational facilities: volleyball, softball. Dances twice a week.

Cold packs for the overactive. Place was noisy.

4.30 – 5 pm. Supper.
In bed by 8 pm.

Some isolation blocks. 'Untidy Wards' for old patients who couldn't control bowels. 'Closed Wards' for escapees, deteriorated psychopaths. 'Violent Wards' for unmanageables.

*

Am walked out of the House of D and put on a north train by H.B. McMurray and Jones. Outside a river can't get out of the rain. Passing wet chicory that lies in the field like the sky. The trees rocks brown ditches falling off the side as we go past. The train in a wet coat. Blue necklace holding my hands together. Going to a pound. My beautiful snout is hit by McMurray for laughing at the rain. My neck is warm is wet and it feels like a shoe stuck in there. T. Jones next to me, the window next to me, McMurray in front of me. His hand came up like magic and got me for laughing as loud as the train. Strangers sitting next to the horizon. Wet in my neck. Teasel in my neck. You see I had an operation on my throat. You see I had a salvation on my throat. A goat put his horn in me and pulled. Let me tell ya, it went winter in there and then it fell apart like mud and they stuck it together with needles and they held me together with clothes.

Am going to the pound. McMurray and Jones holding my hands. Breastless woman in blue pyjamas will be there. Muscles in the arms will be there. Tie. Belt. Boots.

They make me love them. They are the arms looking after me. On the second day they came into my room and took off all my clothes and bent me over a table and broke my anus. They gave me a white dress. They know I am a barber and I didn't tell them I'm a barber. Won't. Can't. Boot in my throat, the food has to climb over it and then go down and meet with all their pals in the stomach. Hi sausage. Hi cabbage. Did yuh see that fuckin·boot. Yeah I nearly turned round 'n went back on the plate. Who is this guy we're in anyway?

The sun comes every day. Save the string. I put it in lines across the room. I watched him creep his body through the grilled windows. When the sun touches the first string wham it is 10 o clock. It is 2 o clock when he touches the second. When the shadow of the first string is under the second string it is 4 o clock. When it reaches the door it will soon be dark.

Laughing in my room. As you try to explain me I will spit you, yellow, out of my mouth.

*

In the summer they were up each day at 4.30. They washed and moved among themselves for an hour and then by 6 they filed in and took forks off the table, ate. At 7 they held the forks above their heads so they could be collected. Meals silent in the mornings and noisy at lunch. That was their only character.

On Monday mornings he cut hair for them. He was never much of a barber but the forms said he was one. So he shaved and cut in a corner of the dining room with an old man who was better than him but who died two years after Bolden arrived. He was asked to train someone new, he didn't react, but a couple of them learned by watching him. One of the patients, Bertram Lord, came every week and tried to get the scissors off him and each day as the shift ended Bolden held up his arm with the scissors and razor and they were collected and locked away.

Lord, who knew of Bolden's reputation, was always trying to persuade him to escape. The noise of Lord so constant it was like wallpaper and Bolden could blot himself against it without even having to turn away the meaning of the words, using the noise as a bark around himself.

Till the day of the escape he had never seen Lord do anything more than talk, so that when Lord saw his chance and without hesitation jumped, Bolden was for the first time impressed. Though not having listened to the shadow who had been using his silence as an oracle, he had no idea what Bertram Lord was up to.

Everyone was jumping on the tables to look. It had begun with Antrim who was getting his weekly needle so he would detour his fits, forget to express them. He had begun to argue with Dr Vernon, some ridiculous reason. The doctors had alternated arms with Antrim who was certain that this week it was supposed to be his left arm and Vernon had begun rolling up the right sleeve. Vernon had put down the needle to calm the furious patient when Lord passing the open room had leapt in scooped up the needle and thrown his other arm around the doctor's neck.

He dragged the doctor down the hall with the needle held inches from the eye, he forced the guards to open the doors. The two guards hesitated and Lord, nervous, tightened his fist round the glass syringe so much the glass tubing was crushed. Still he held onto the needle, gently now, like a dart, and the guard seeing it not even waver from the doctor's eye, opened the doors. Lord then called out for others to follow, he called out Bolden's name again and again but his friend was now sitting on the barber chair watching it all, waiting for the next customer who was somewhere on a table leaping up and down. So Lord went out. He was away for two days loose in the town of Jackson and then was brought back and beaten. He had a limp, said he almost broke his ankle going over a fence. But that wasn't the cause. In his time out he had separated precisely the bottom circle from a bottle of Coca-Cola. He had ground it into a sharp disc and he kept it hidden under the instep of his left foot. He had it there in his tight shoe. He had his weapon and he'd come back for Bolden.

Selections from *A Brief History of East Louisiana State Hospital* by Lionel Gremillion

Hospital was opened in the year 1848. 87 patients transferred from the Charity Hospital in New Orleans.

1853. A minority report from a special committee stated patients in direst poverty and lacked sufficient food. Dinner consisted of a tin cupful of soup, meat about the size of a hen's egg, and a small piece of bread. Breakfast was bread and coffee. Supper was bread and tea. Women patients not properly clothed. Cells had no heat.

1857. J.D. Barkdull made Superintendent. First time the institution was under the control of a medical man.

1861. Hospital included thirty-six girls, mostly under twelve years of age.

1855. Dysentery swept crowded wards and it was stated that 'the diseased patients fell like grass before the scythe.'

1859. Some of the causes of insanity were listed as: ill health, loss of property, excessive use of tobacco, dissipation, domestic affliction, epilepsy, masturbation, home-sickness, injury of the head. The largest category was 'unknown'.

1864. Supt. Barkdull was shot and killed in the streets of Jackson by a yankee soldier.

During the Civil War it was almost impossible to get food or water supplies to the hospital.

1882. Introduction of occupational therapy. Patients assigned to make moss mattresses.

1902-1904.	1397 patients. 490 were black. The Hospital purchased iron lavatories and toilets. A 20′ fountain was constructed on the lawn in front of the female building and stocked with gold and silver fish.
1910-1912.	1496 patients. The death rate was 11% per year. A moving picture machine was purchased for the amusement of the patients. A hearse was made at the hospital. A motor car was purchased to convey seven to eight passengers to and from the station.
1912-1914.	The Hospital Band played every afternoon on the hospital lawn from 2 pm till 4 pm. 1650 patients. Wasserman tests were taken for the first time from 1924 onwards. Bolden given test. Negative.
1924 onwards.	Dr T.J. Perkins made Superintendent. 2100 patients.
	1931. Buddy Bolden dies.
	1948. The Medcraft Shock Machine was purchased. Still in use today.

*

Willy Cornish

Then everyone was becoming famous. Jazz was now history. The library people were doing recordings and interviews. They didn't care who it was that talked they just got them talking. Like Amacker, Woodman, Porteous, anybody. They didn't ask what happened to his wife, his children, and no one knew about the Brewitts. All I had of Buddy was the picture here. Webb gave that to me. I never wanted to talk about him.

Didn't know what to say. He had all that talent and wisdom he stole and learnt from people and then smashed it, smashed it like ice coming onto the highway off a truck. What did he see with all that? What good is all that if we can't learn or know? I think Bellocq corrupted him with that mean silence so Buddy went and Bellocq stayed here shocked by his going and Buddy gone for two years then coming back and gentle with us till he had to go ... crazy in front of children and Nora and everyone.

Then jesus that, *jesus* that hospital and the company there which he slid through like a pin in the blood. With all his friends outside like they were on a grandstand watching him and when they began to realize he would never come out then all the people he hardly knew, all the fools, beginning to talk about him ...

*

In the room there is the air
                                                            and there is the corner
and there is the corner and there is the corner
and there is the corner.

If you don't shake, don't get no cake.

Bella Davenport married Willy Cornish in 1922.
Cornish 6′ 3″ – 297 lbs.
'When I married him he was healthy as a pig'

Cornish had his first stroke on Rampart and
Julien while playing. Arm paralysed.
Bella questioned about those Cornish
had played with –

'He and Buddy were just like that'
&
'All of them mostly lost their minds'

*

When protests began over guard rapes, bad plumbing, labour, lack of heat, the patients organised a strike. This did nothing. They then cut their tendons. Not Bolden, who sublime took rapes from what he thought were ladies in blue pyjamas. And work as his duty to the sun. Bertram Lord walked down the hall and slid the coke bottom under each door to the patients. They took the sharpened glass, cut their tendon, and passed it back. Bolden who saw the foreign weapon enter his room left his window where he was waiting for morning, heard the whispered order on the other side of the wood, peered at it, touched it with his foot and pushed it back slowly to Lord who eventually covered 28 doors.

In the morning men were found heels bandaged in their nightshirts and naked when the doors opened. The sun fell on Bolden's waiting face, he smiled, walked out spry and was almost alone at breakfast where he met his visitor again, this morning as a brilliant lush bar of light that lay in an oblong stretch nearly touching his plate. So bright it showed him the textures of the old fork-scarred table. He almost didn't want to eat today. He kept putting down his spoon in the tin bowl and placing his hand over the warm yellow of his friend and his friend magically managed to put his light over Bolden's hand simultaneously, so that it was kept warm. Later in the day he moved following his path. He washed his face in the travelling spokes of light, bathing and drying his mouth nose forehead and cheeks in the heat. All day. Blessed by the visit of his friend.

*

Webb in town years later, 1924, talked to Bella Davenport, Willy Cornish's wife then, Bella Cornish then, in the corner of a loud party. Talking and eventually sliding onto the subject of Bolden. Webb said he had been an old friend of his. This was the year Tom Pickett was shot and killed on Poydras Street. The party was on Napoleon, everybody crowded into two floors and stairs and on the steps outside. Webb back here after many years, standing beside Bella Davenport and not too interested until she said she was Bella Cornish rattling her white china pearls, and Webb looking at her and recognizing they were all growing old, the lines deep and thin and dark on their faces.

So it must have been over Pickett's death that they got onto Bolden. He and Willy were just like that, she said. Sitting with her on the bend of the stairs he said that Buddy's death had surprised him, he'd always expected Bolden to jump out of his silence when he got bored, shit I was sure he was just hiding you know hiding from us all and that he'd put on a red shirt and come back, yeah, Nora's letter surprised me alright, I'd been going in every few months to visit though he said nothing and then she writes not to bother anymore because Buddy died, how things get to you huh. Looking up then because the rattling of pearls had stopped and Bella Cornish was not moving. *But he's not dead,* whispered. He's still at the hospital, the state hospital, he's still there, heaven. When did Nora write you?

Eight years ago.

He's still there, eighteen years now. Willy saw him a year ago. He does nothing, nothing at all. Never speaks, goes around touching things. One of the doctors told Willy who had to pretend to be his brother. Willy sat in the hall all day to talk to the doctor and Willy just getting over his stroke, heaven, they told him Buddy touches things, there are about twenty things he will touch and he goes from one to the next, that's all. Won't talk, do you know they even have a band but he has nothing to do with it, was cutting hair but that stopped a while back. Now this touching thing. Willy nursing his soft hand goes all the way to the hospital and stays in places like Vachery overnight to get there and Buddy don't say a thing to him. And he and Willy were just like *that*. Don't even pretend to know who he is. The doctor says that most of the patients don't know who their visitors are but they pretend they do so they have company but Buddy won't. Willy walked round with him while he went about, like doing a tour or inspection of the place, the taps on the bath, the door frame, benches, things like that.

She talked on and on repeating herself and her descriptions, going back to things she'd mentioned and retelling them in greater detail for Webb. Who could not talk just strained his body and head against the wall behind him as if he were trying to escape the smell of her words as if the air from her talking came into his mouth and filled it puffed it up with poison so the brain was put to sleep and he could do nothing with it only react in his flesh. She talked on not knowing he had brought Buddy home, instead, seeing the effect of her words, she whispered on bending nearer to him like a lover surrounded by the loud moving of the party against them telling him again and again *he touches things*, like taps first the hot water one and then the cold, which was not true for there were only cold water taps at the East Louisiana State Hospital, but she continued to describe – as fascinated by that strange act as if it was the luxurious itch under a scab. While he arched away his body stiff and hard trying to break through the wall every nerve on the outside as if Bella's mouth was crawling over him, and his unknown flesh had taken over, and crashed fast down the stairs stepping on hands and glasses almost running over the bodies on the crowded stairs smiling and excusing himself out loud I gotta throw up 'scuse me 'scuse me, but knowing there was nothing to come up at all.

Bella watched the flapping body on its way down the stairs and noticing now the damp mark on her right where his sweat had in those few minutes gone through his skin his shirt his java jacket and driven itself onto the wall.

*

Frank Amacker Interviews. Transcript Digest. Tulane Library. Also present William Russell, Allan and Sandra Jaffe, Richard B. Allen.

Reel 1. June 21, 1965

Plays (almost immediately) old rag with wide arm spread. He cannot remember the name of the rag. He discusses his prowess in playing with hands far apart. He'd like to bet that nobody can beat him at that. He now says that he made up the last song.

He then talks about this wide arm spread being the natural way of playing the piano. He then talks about the public acceptance of pianists who can't play as well as he. Asked how old he is, he replies that he was seventy-five years old on March 22, 1965. AJ asks for 'My Josephine'. FA plays 'Moonlight on the Ganges'. He says he and Jelly Roll Morton hung around the BIG 25 together. He was playing there on the night of the Billy Phillips killing at the 101 Ranch. Gyp the Blood killed Billy Phillips right in front of his own bar at 4.20 am on Easter Monday and then went across the street and killed Harry Parker. The salary was $1.00 to $1.50 a night, plus tips. Money was worth a lot more then. He explains the meaning of 'Lagniappe'. He explains the term 'can rusher'.

END OF REEL ONE

Reel 2.

There follows a discussion of waltzes. He says he can play 'The Sweetheart of Sigma Chi' and 'Schubert's Serenade'. WR asks for the latter, and FA plays 'Drigo's Serenade'. He became quite wealthy he says, but lost all of it. At one time he owned five places. At one time he had a bar and a restaurant. The welfare department has all the records of his former wealth.

END OF REEL TWO.

Reel 3.

He plays 'The House Got Ready'. He plays the Amos 'n' Andy theme song. Next a slow rag with wide arm spread again. (Some of his rags have obscene titles. He would not give them in front of SJ or RBA.) FA says he used to play thousands of rags. He doesn't know how to play Jelly Roll Morton's 'The Pearls'. Then he plays and sings 'I'll see you in my dreams'. Asks for a little shot.

END OF REEL THREE

Reel 1. Digest Retype. July 1, 1960

Frank Amacker born in New Orleans, March 22, 1890. He began playing music when he was sixteen, playing in the District. His first instrument was piano, he later took up guitar. RBA asks if FA ever played (Tony Jackson's) 'The Naked Dance'. FA says he played many naked dances, but the piano player was just supposed to play, keeping his eyes on the keyboard and not looking at the whores. FA then says that it is God's will that he looks as young as he is today, that it must be that he is being saved for something special by God.

He says he knows he could play most of the things he hears on television, that all he needs is a chance.

END OF REEL ONE.

Reel 2.

[No interesting information]

Reel 3.

FA says a really good singer, like Perry Como, should be able to take the song he now plays, which he composed, and make a hit out of it. FA then says that A.J. Piron heard him playing the song, years ago, and told him it was the most beautiful song he ever heard, that he would write it down and make him famous. The name of the song is 'All the boys got to love me, that's all'. Johnny St Cyr wrote the words and Piron wrote it down. All the people in the District praised the song. It was the most unusual blues you ever heard. It was so sad. It's about a man who takes his girl to a dance. The girl starts flirting with another man. He doesn't start a fight, but takes her home and sings this song. (FA plays and sings). The lyrics are full of regret, he tells her he is sorry he met her, among other things, and finishes by saying he is going to take her into the woods and shoot her. He kills her but he still loves her and he tells the undertaker to be very careful with his beautiful baby.

END OF REEL THREE

Reel 4.

FA answers questions about good trumpet players by saying that Buddy Bolden was the loudest. Freddy Keppard was a master, and so was Manuel Perez, but the most masterful master of all was James McNeil who was college trained. In contrast Bolden played this 'old lowdown music'. FA says he remembers 'Funky Butt' (also known as 'Buddy Bolden's Blues'). FA does not remember August Russell. He says Johnny Delpit was a good violinist. He says Frank DeLandry (or D.Landry or Delandro?) was the greatest guitarist he ever heard. He says all the guitars were buried when DeLandry died.

END OF REEL FOUR

---

*

T. Jones

'The train he was on – sorry, let me start again. The train journey took up the first 100 miles. Nobody knew who he was so there was no problem. The surgery round his throat done in the House of D covered with bandage. Above it his emotionless face looking straight ahead – they all do that, as if showing how they can control themselves. Black coat, open shirt. And all day the river at our side, Mississippi, like a friend travelling with him, like an audience watching Huck Finn going by train to hell. Oh sure I read too you know. I can see the joke. I know he was important, but he was also sick and crazy...

At Baton Rouge the bandage was full of red though he had hardly moved. I gave him a cloth to cover it. Whole trip went well. No trouble. He must have been tired from the operation the day before. From Baton Rouge we took the wagon up through Sunshine, Vachery, and Slaughter. Forty-eight miles. Again he was very calm. North of Slaughter McMurray and I wanted to swim. It was hot. We stopped and found a small river. We got him down off the wagon and took him the 100 yards to the water and he just stood on the bank. He watched while we took turns swimming. That was the fifth of June, so he was admitted late that day. We never saw him after that. We put him in the chair in the Superintendent's office, got the papers signed and left him with them.'

They had gone through the country that Audubon drew. Twenty miles from the green marshes where he waited for birds to fly onto and bend the branch right in front of his eyes. Mr Audubon drew until lunchtime, sitting with his assistant who frequently travelled with him. The meal was consumed around a hamper, a bottle of wine was opened with as little noise as possible in order not to scare the wildlife away.

*

I sit with this room. With the grey walls that darken into corner. And one window with teeth in it. Sit so still you can hear your hair rustle in your shirt. Look away from the window when clouds and other things go by. Thirty-one years old. There are no prizes.